The Thought Stealers

TO ALICE,

ENJOY THE STORY,

Guy WL

The Thought Stealers

Guy Wilson

TS Publishing

TS Publishing

The Thought Stealers

Published 2008 by TS Publishing

Copyright © Guy Wilson 2008

Author information at www.guywilson.co.uk

Cover illustration by Caroline Crossland

ISBN: 978-0-9559964-0-5

Chapter one

A nnie Short stared in horror at the ghastly thing happening to the young boy standing in front of her. It was revolting. Dark like a shadow, matter was oozing out of his nostrils before hanging in the air around his body in a thick cloud.

Unable to breathe, let alone move, Annie just watched. *What's happening?* her mind screamed. *This is awful!*

The boy continued to stand in a trance-like state, his blue eyes wide, vacant, before all of a sudden he shuddered, as more and more dark vapour surged out through his nose. If his curly short brown hair had been standing on end she would have guessed an electric current was passing directly through him.

Annie wanted to scream her head off, but her mouth wouldn't allow it. Instead, she just stood there, transfixed, whilst the cloud changed shape.

In no time at all its outline became sharp, like a predator's teeth, before it started to pulsate.

"Annabelle Short," the mysterious shape rasped, floating on the light breeze towards her.

Hearing this, Annie couldn't believe it. The shadowy vision seemed to be alive.

"You've been lucky this time," the threatening cloud growled. "But have no doubt, before this day's over I'll have fed on your thoughts until all that is left inside your mind is an empty space."

1

Fearing she wouldn't make it to her eleventh birthday she flinched, before all of a sudden it abruptly shot into the air way above her head and disappeared into the thick sea of trees that loomed over the pathway.

No sooner had the eerie creature vanished than Annie regained the use of her arms and legs. "What on earth was that?" she gasped, her hands trembling.

"What was what?" a voice cut in.

Her heart pounding, she looked over and noticed the boy had snapped out of his trance and was staring directly at her, puzzlement written across his face.

Annie didn't know what to say.

"What was what?" the boy asked again.

"Err… I'm not sure," Annie muttered, her legs now feeling like jelly.

As though completely unaffected by what had happened, the boy rushed over. "Are you okay?" he asked.

Annie struggled to get her words out. "I-I-I'm not sure," she whispered. "I just watched a shadowy creature come out of your nose, before it drifted towards me and threatened to feed on my thoughts."

The boy gasped, grabbing his nose before running his hands over his face to make sure it was still in one piece. "It was inside me?" he cried.

Annie was about to reply, but stopped.

Ever since the death of her parents she had rejected tales of ghosts and monsters as nothing more than stories to scare naughty children and that was why she was now having trouble believing her eyes. Because of this she suddenly changed her tune: "I must have imagined it."

The boy took her word for it and started to act as though nothing odd had taken place. "Hey, my name's Fred. Fred Greene," he said. "I live here on the campsite. So what's your name?"

"Huh?" Annie whispered, still thinking about the horrible apparition.

"What's your name?" Fred repeated.

"Annie," she finally replied, brushing a loose strand of light wavy brown hair behind her left ear. "Annie Short."

"Hi, Annie," he said, smiling. "I guess you're staying at the campsite then?"

"Y-y-yeah," she stuttered, "I'm here for the week with my aunt. We've come down from Leicester."

"So what do you think of the sunny Devonshire town of Brixham then?" the ten-year-old boy asked.

"It's great," she declared, looking down at the cove at the bottom of the path. Although it had just gone six in the morning, the sun glistened off the water, making her squint.

"It's going to be another scorching summer's day!" Fred exclaimed. "Great weather for swimming in the sea and getting a tan."

Hearing this, Annie suddenly snapped out of her daze and kicked herself for forgetting to apply suntan lotion before leaving the caravan. An hour in the sun would leave her freckly face bright red and sore.

"So why are you up so early?" Fred then enquired. "Surely you should be sleeping in until at least eight, like all the other guests."

Rather than answer the question, the vision of the shadowy creature flashed in front of her mind's eye. It was repulsive – a sinister cloud of dark matter with sharp edges and an air of menace about it. She rubbed her eyes, trying to get the image out of her mind. But it wouldn't leave. The creature's words then bounced around inside her head. *Before this day's over I'll have fed on your thoughts until all that is left inside your mind is an empty space,* it growled.

"Annie, you okay?" Fred asked.

Annie snapped out of her day-mare. "I'm not sure," she muttered. Because the vision had seemed so real, she wondered whether it was possible that the monster could actually have existed.

Wanting to know one way or the other, she asked, "Fred, do you remember seeing the big dark cloud ooze out of your nose?"

The boy shook his head. "No."

"You don't remember anything bizarre happening?" she probed further.

Fred shook his head again. "All I remember is deciding to go for a short walk to get some fresh air, since I couldn't sleep, and then seeing you."

This was what she wanted to hear. Of course he hadn't remembered anything weird happening, because she had imagined the whole thing.

As for how real the monster seemed... *It must be the sea air,* she thought, remembering what a local fisherman had said a day earlier. The man had told Annie and her aunt that the air around the coast plays havoc with the senses of people visiting from the Midlands.

But Annie had to be sure though, so she asked, "You're okay now?"

Fred smiled. "Yeah."

"No headaches?" she enquired.

The boy shook his head.

"Do you feel dizzy or have the urge to puke your guts up?" she continued.

"Nope," Fred replied.

"Well that settles it," Annie said. "The sea air's been playing tricks on my eyes."

Fred smiled again. "But it would've been cool if a monster or a ghost had been inside me!" he exclaimed. "Don't you think?"

Annie screwed up her face. "That would never happen, since monsters and ghosts don't exist," she replied.

"Don't believe in weird things, huh?" Fred asked.

"No way," Annie insisted.

"Well I guess that's your view," Fred muttered, holding up his hands. "So why are you up so early?" he asked again, getting away from a possible argument.

Annie was pulled back to reality. "I wanted to check out the rock pools before all of the sunbathers scare the sea life away. I was planning to make notes on what I find," she explained, pulling a pencil and notebook from the pocket of her favourite, over-worn, red shorts that didn't by any stretch of the imagination match her green T-shirt and deep green eyes. In fact, if it wasn't for her slight frame and long hair, at a glance she could be mistaken for a badly dressed boy.

"Does this interest you?" she asked.

Fred shook his head. "Not really my thing. I prefer computers and bike rides," he pointed out. "So I guess I'll leave you to it as I'm ready to get a couple more hours shut eye."

"Sure," Annie said. "Maybe I'll see you around."

Fred waved before wandering off up the path.

Having chatted to Fred, Annie felt confident she had imagined the shadowy creature. If the monster had actually oozed out of Fred's nose, then he would have been acting strange instead of carrying on like nothing was in the slightest bit wrong.

But what if it did actually happen? she wondered, walking down the steep pathway.

"No!" she argued with her own mind. "Ghosts and monsters don't exist!"

Chapter two

While Annie crouched on the rocks, looking down at the small pools containing dozens of shrimps darting around, a strange sensation washed over her. It felt like someone was watching her.

Feeling jittery, she snapped her head round and looked, putting her hand over her brow and squinting through the glare of the sun.

But there was no one about. All she could see was the water lapping at the jagged rocks of the cove and a few seagulls circling in the blue summer sky, searching for fish below.

This is stupid, she thought. *First I imagined seeing a horrible monster, now I'm thinking someone's watching me.*

But no sooner had she returned to her project than the sensation came back. It was as though a pair of eyes were boring into the back of her head.

She snapped her head round again. "Who's there?" she demanded, her body shivering despite the hot weather. "Fred, is that you? If you're around here it's not funny – just show yourself!"

But again the young girl couldn't see another soul.

The person could be in the water! she suddenly thought.

But apart from a trawler leisurely sailing into the harbour several hundred feet outside the cove with seagulls following it, hoping to feed on some of the discarded fish, the water was empty.

She returned to her examination of the small pool. But before long a cold chill again swept over her body. However, this time she didn't feel like she was being watched. Instead a woman's voice seemed to float on the light breeze. *If you want to know what happened to that boy, go to the town library and you'll find the answers there,* the voice said.

Startled, Annie looked round again. "Who said that?" she yelled.

But again there was no one there.

There's a great evil present here, the voice whispered, seeming to come from everywhere. *I need your help to stop it. Go to the library and you'll find the answers there.*

This time Annie's heart stepped into overdrive. Things were getting too creepy so she jumped to her feet and charged across the rocks, careful not to slip on the seaweed or lose her footing on the uneven surface. She didn't stop until she was inside her caravan back at the campsite.

"Aunt Grace, Aunt Grace!" she bellowed, bursting into her aunt's bedroom and diving on her bed. "The most horrible things have just happened!"

Annie's aunt awoke with a start, sitting bolt upright, as though a pair of jump leads had been attached to her ears.

"Aunt Grace!" Annie shrieked, shaking her, causing the forty-year-old woman's red hair to dance around like flames. "You'll never guess what just happened!"

Aunt Grace rubbed her tired green eyes. "What's wrong?" she groaned.

"First I imagined seeing a massive shadow come out of a boy's nose and then someone spoke to me, but when I looked round there was no one there!" she explained.

Hearing this, Aunt Grace raised an eyebrow right before a small smile crept across her face, which was even frecklier than her niece's. She then rubbed Annie's arm before tidying her hair, which had got messy in all of the excitement. "I think this is the product of a child's imagination," she said softly.

"No, you don't understand," Annie insisted, her heart hammering away. "First I thought I imagined seeing a horrible monster, but when I also heard a ghostly voice now I think the monster might have actually been real."

"Annie," Aunt Grace said, "I thought you didn't believe in monsters and ghosts. I thought you believed in nothing other than what you learnt down at junior science club."

Annie was flustered. "I know, but now I'm not so sure," she insisted. "The monster and voice seemed so real."

Aunt Grace continued to smile. "Annie, although these things seemed real, what would a good junior scientist do? They wouldn't jump straight to the conclusion that it was a monster. Would they?"

Annie's hands were still trembling. "No," she replied, knowing her aunt was probably right.

"So what would a junior scientist do?" Aunt Grace asked a second time, calming her niece down.

In all the excitement Annie hadn't had time to stop and think. But now her aunt had steadied her nerves she replied, "A good scientist would look for a rational, logical explanation."

"That's better," Aunt Grace agreed. "Now what would a good scientist do next?"

Annie had to think, but she knew there was only one thing she could do to get to the bottom of this: find Fred and ask him a few more questions.

Chapter three

It was nine o'clock in the morning by the time Annie tracked Fred down. He was in the campsite dining hall.

The moment she walked through the wooden doors the young girl noticed the massive place was a hive of activity. There was a long queue for the canteen, which had dinner ladies serving up platefuls of slop, and nearly all of the benches were filled with people troughing down as much food that their mouths would allow. Annie reckoned they wanted to dash off as quickly as possible to spend the day at the beach baking in the sun, just to come back bright red and sore.

Annie peered at the crowd and quickly spied her target. The ten-year-old boy was sitting on his own, devouring a plateful of bacon and eggs.

She dashed through the crowded hall and sat across the table from him.

"Fred," she said.

He didn't look up. Instead he continued to fill his mouth, forcing a fork full of bacon and eggs between his lips. But it was far too much and bits fell back onto his plate.

"Fred!" she repeated in a loud whisper.

Finally he looked up. "Annie!" he garbled, spraying bits of food over her in the process.

"Thanks," she muttered, wiping her face.

"Sorry," he mumbled, wiping a bit of yolk from his lips.

She glanced from side to side, not wanting anyone else to hear. From her aunt's reaction she was certain that if anyone else overheard what she was about to say, they'd think she was truly mad and would need locking up.

She leaned in. "Fred," she whispered, "I need to talk to you."

"What about?" he replied, again covering her in some of the contents of his mouth.

Annie wiped the food from her face a second time. "I need to talk to you about this morning."

"What about this morning?" he garbled, spraying food everywhere, some of it going down the front of his T-shirt and onto his shorts.

This time Annie put her hand up as a shield. "Can you remember what happened?"

"Of course," he replied. "You said a big shadow came out of my nose. Why?"

"Yeah, but do you actually remember the shadow itself?" she asked.

Fred shook his head. "Like I said earlier, all I remember is getting out of bed, going for a walk and then seeing you. Why do you ask?" he enquired again.

"No reason," she said.

Although Fred saying he hadn't seen the monster should have meant that it was nothing more than a really vivid product of her imagination, she still felt odd. There still wasn't an explanation for the voice she heard.

Fred noticed Annie's peculiar expression. "What's wrong?"

Annie didn't answer. She was concerned about the possibility that the odd thing that she thought she had imagined might just have actually occurred. This worried her, because she didn't fancy a monster feeding on her thoughts until there was nothing left inside her head.

As she walked out of the hall and into the hot summer air, the voice returned. Again it came from all around. *Annie, if you want to know what this is all about then go to the town library. You'll find the answers there.*

"Who said that?" she yelled, looking at the people milling around the campsite.

"Who said what?" a voice asked from behind. It was Fred.

Annie turned round. "Didn't you hear that?"

Fred put his hands up; they were covered in tomato ketchup and egg yolk. "Hear what?"

"I keep hearing a voice," Annie explained. "It keeps telling me to go to the library."

"Okay, I think you might be going mad," Fred commented, before licking the tomato ketchup and egg yolk off his hands.

Annie's frustration was noticeable. "I know. These things I'm seeing and hearing shouldn't be happening. They don't exist!"

"Well you know if it helps," Fred suggested, "we could always try and get to the bottom of this mystery. You know, find out what the strange shadow was that came out of my nose."

"There's no point," Annie insisted. "It wasn't real."

Fred wasn't taking no for an answer. "Yeah, but there'll be no harm in trying to solve this mystery. Besides if we don't find anything it'll be fun to hang out for the day. Maybe I could show you around Brixham."

Annie was slightly taken aback. "I'm not sure. I wouldn't want to take you away from your friends. You probably already have plans to play on the beach or go for a bike ride."

"No plans," Fred smiled. "I could show you where the library is."

Annie scratched her head. On the one hand she wanted to get to the bottom of this mystery and prove to herself that it wasn't a monster or a ghost that she had seen, but on the other she didn't really want to take Fred away from his friends.

Although it would be good to hang out with Fred, since back home she didn't have many friends to hang out with as no one shared her interests. She finally spoke: "Let me think about it."

Chapter four

Half an hour had passed and Annie hadn't thought about anything else for the whole time. *Okay, so a shadow came out of Fred's nose. But that doesn't mean it was a ghost or a monster,* she thought. *I still don't believe in ghosts and monsters.*

But now she wasn't so sure.

No! she thought. *There has to be a sensible scientific reason for all of this and there's one way to prove it. I've got to go to the library.*

She looked over to her aunt, who was sitting outside the caravan on a deckchair, soaking up the morning rays and reading through a short story she had just finished writing. She was a freelance writer and made a living having her stories published in magazines and books.

"Aunt Grace," she said, "is it okay if I spend the day with a young boy I've just met?"

Her aunt removed her sunglasses, exposing the pair of deep green eyes that she shared with Annie's mother, and looked up from her story. "A young boy?"

"Yeah, his name's Fred," Annie explained. "He lives here on the campsite."

"I thought you wanted to take another canoeing lesson today?" Aunt Grace asked.

"I did, but Fred wants to show me around Brixham," Annie explained, having spent the last few days on the water in a small canoe. "I think it'll be fun."

Aunt Grace looked back down at her story. "Okay, but make sure you ring me at lunchtime to tell me where you are and that you're back by tea-time."

Annie smiled, knowing that her aunt was good to her. She wasn't overly strict, but always made sure she stayed out of trouble. "Thanks," Annie said.

"Oh and remember it's the firework display this evening and the fair," Aunt Grace pointed out. "Now I don't usually spoil you, but don't eat too much today because you'll need to save room for hot dogs and candyfloss."

The smile across Annie's face grew larger, remembering that they were going to the fair before watching the fireworks that marked the end of Brixham's summer regatta. "Thanks," she said, kissing her aunt on the cheek, before pinching some of her aunt's suntan lotion and applying it to her body.

She then rummaged around the pockets of her shorts, which were filled with sand and dirt, for her bike lock keys. She found them and unlocked her bike before riding off.

In no time at all Annie was knocking on Fred's door and after the third bang it was answered by his mother, Mrs Greene.

"Hi, is Fred around?" she asked the lady, who looked very similar to her son. She had curly brown hair and sea blue eyes. She also had a kind smile.

"You must be Annie," Mrs Greene said, before bellowing, "Poppet, there's someone here to see you!"

A small smirk inched across Annie's face. *Poppet,* she thought.

Fred eventually appeared. "Annie," he muttered, stunned, "what're you doing here?"

"I was wondering whether you wanted to spend the day with me?" she asked. "That's only if I'm not going to be taking you away from your friends."

Fred smiled. "I'd love to!"

Before Annie could speak, Fred's mother turned to her son. "I told you, you did the right thing," she said, ruffling up his hair.

"Mum," he protested, fighting her off, "stop it! I'm ten years old. You're embarrassing me."

The boy fought off his mother. "Come on, let's get out of here before she tries to feed me my lunch or give me a bath," he mumbled to Annie.

Okay," Annie replied, wondering what Mrs Greene meant by her comment that Fred had done the right thing. It seemed odd.

"Sorry about that," the boy said. "Mum always treats me like that; it's a bit annoying."

"Fred, if I were in your shoes I'd lap it up. You really don't know how lucky you are," she said.

18

"Now get your bike, Poppet, we've got a mystery to solve."

Chapter five

Annie and Fred arrived at the library in the centre of Brixham town. Fred had kept up on his bike, which was a top of the range Challenger mountain bike with twenty-one gears, mud guards and suspension. It was so much better than Annie's second-hand Raleigh that only had eighteen gears, no suspension and a thin layer of rust on the joints.

"So what now?" Fred asked between breaths.

"I'm not sure," Annie replied. "The voice told me that the answer to this mystery would be contained inside the library."

"I hate to rain on your parade," Fred argued, "but whereabouts? It could be anywhere. It'll take a lifetime to search through the thousands of books."

Annie groaned. "I'm starting to think it was a bad idea bringing you along."

He held up his hands. "I'm just saying, this ghostly voice was a little bit vague."

"I reckon that the best thing to do will be to go inside," she suggested, locking up her bike and then walking towards the building. "Maybe we'll see the answer straight away."

Once inside, Annie noticed that the library was state-of-the-art. It had two floors, a new lick of paint on the walls, a clean carpet, several computers in the reference section and friendly faced librarians. In fact, it was worlds away from the one back home, which could only be described as a shed with a leaky roof that was run by a bony old witch who spoke in a high pitched cackle, constantly telling her to be quiet.

"So what did your mum mean earlier when she said you'd done the right thing?" Annie asked, shivering from the cold blast coming out of the air-conditioning unit.

"Nothing," Fred replied, before changing the subject back to the mystery at hand. "So what's the plan?"

But Annie didn't answer, because suddenly a sensation hit her like a bolt of lightening.

"Are you okay?" Fred asked.

"I'm not sure," she replied, feeling like she wasn't in complete control of her arms and legs.

"You look like you've seen a ghost," he noted.

Before she could answer, a force took over her body and pulled her up the stairs. She was powerless to stop herself barging through the people coming down the other way.

"Sorry!" Annie shrieked, charging up the stairs, unable to stop her body. She was moving like an out of control robot.

Fred struggled to keep up, as Annie barged more people out of the way. "Sorry!" he yelled to the angry face of a man who'd just had a pile of books knocked out of his hands.

Once on the top floor, Annie stopped dead in her tracks.

Fred caught up. "What now?" he panted.

21

"I don't know," she replied, her arms shooting out in front. "I'm not in control of my body."

Suddenly the force acted again and this time her body moved through the aisles of books, towards the end shelves. She stopped in front of the section headed *Local ghost tales.*

"Oh, no," she muttered. This wasn't what she wanted.

Once more, Fred caught up. He then realised what section they were in. He looked at her. "Still don't believe in ghosts?"

Annie thought she had regained the use of her limbs, but she was wrong. Her right hand pointed in the direction of one of the books. It was a leather bound book covered in dust.

"I think that's the one we want," Fred suggested. "It looks like it hasn't been read in years."

"I think you're right," she whispered, powerless to prevent her hand pulling her whole body towards the book.

Her hand then picked the book off the shelf, before her body pushed her in the direction of a table, nearly knocking Fred over in the process.

Finally Annie regained the use of her limbs, as she looked at the book now resting on the table in front.

In all the excitement, Annie touched her dry lips with her trembling fingers. *This shouldn't be happening!* her mind cried. *I believe in science, not ghosts and monsters!*

But it was happening and although she felt too scared to look at the book, curiosity drew her green eyes to the name on the cover.

Fred sat down next to her before she read what was printed on the cover.

But there was a problem.

Although she could see it had been written by a woman called *Eira Flynn,* she couldn't make out the title. It had been scratched off.

Chapter six

Annie looked closely at the cover. It definitely looked like it hadn't been read in years.

"Open it," Fred whispered, his voice unsteady.

Annie barely heard him; she was mesmerised by the book. *What force dragged me here?* and *Why have I been chosen for this?* were a couple of questions flying around in her mind.

"Open it," he repeated.

"Okay," she replied, her hands trembling. She pulled open the cover and looked inside.

But what they found left them bewildered. The book was empty.

"Huh?" Annie grunted. "I don't get it."

Fred was bemused. "Maybe there's a secret compartment somewhere," he suggested, picking up the book and examining it.

"I don't think so," Annie sighed, looking at the book's spine. "I think someone's beaten us here and ripped the pages out. Clearly someone doesn't want us reading the contents."

"Well that's just great!" Fred snapped, dropping what was left of the book on the table.

"I guess that's just about the end of the mystery for us. Back to the campsite, I suppose," Annie muttered, getting up from her seat. "Fancy going to the beach?"

Don't give up now, the ghostly voice suddenly whispered. *You don't have much time. A great evil is planning something horrible.*

"I heard the voice again," Annie whispered, shivering.

"Well, what did it say?" Fred demanded.

"It told me not to give up and that a great evil's planning something horrible."

"A great evil?" Fred asked.

"Yeah," she said, sitting back down and scratching her head. "I wish this person would show herself and give us all the answers. Without this book we don't have any clues."

"Maybe we do," Fred cut in, a wry smile creeping across his face.

"Like what?" she asked.

"I knew it was a great idea I came along!" he exclaimed, picking up the book. He jumped to his feet and charged down the stairs to the computers.

"What do you mean?" she asked, trying to keep up as well as trying not to barge people out of the way.

Fred sat himself in front of a computer. "Everyone thinks I'm a mummy's boy, but I spend all my time in front of the computer at home and I've become really good on it," he explained whilst furiously typing away at the keyboard.

In a matter of moments Annie watched Fred bring up a search engine that gave access to Torbay council's library database.

"What are you doing?" she asked, puzzled by his odd behaviour.

"This book was in the section entitled *Local ghost stories,* so that means the author's likely to live nearby. If that's the case, then maybe her address is on this database," he suggested, punching several more commands into the keyboard.

A search box appeared in the top right-hand corner of the screen. He clicked on it, typed in the name *Eira Flynn* and pressed enter.

In an instant, the pair watched Eira Flynn's details come up on the screen.

"This can't be legal?" Annie whispered.

Fred didn't answer, he just produced a mischievous smile.

Annie read the list of the author's previous work, which included *How to Catch a Thought Person, How to Stop Your Thoughts Being Stolen, Ten Things Not to Do When a Thought Person Is in Your House* and *How Holding Your Nose Will Protect You from A Nasty Thought Person.*

"I underestimated you," she said. "A computer whiz, huh?"

"That's me," he explained cheerfully, not looking away from the screen. "Your typical nerd – great on a computer, but rubbish at sport."

"Oh come on," Annie urged. "Every young lad's good at football."

Fred finally looked up. "Not me," he smiled. "I realised that earlier this year."

"How come?" she asked.

"Let's just say I was a part of the Brixham Crickets Under Tens football team last season and I only got to play two games," he explained. "The rest of the time I was a sub."

"That's okay," Annie said. "Only getting a couple of games doesn't mean you're rubbish."

"Annie," Fred explained, "in those matches I scored three own goals and accidentally gave one of my defenders a broken arm."

There was a stunned silence for several moments. Annie didn't know much about football, but what she did know was that wasn't at all good. Finally she spoke. "Oh well, I guess your talents lie elsewhere."

Instead of carrying on the conversation the young boy then clicked on Eira's name and the author's details appeared on the screen. "It says that she's a scientist who spent most of her life studying Thought People. These books appear to be products of her research."

"What are Thought People?" Annie asked.

"One moment," Fred replied, before reading further. "It doesn't say, but it says that to protect yourself from a nasty one you must pinch your fingers over your nose to stop them going up through your nostrils and into your head."

He looked at Annie. "Do you think it was a nasty Thought Person that came out of my nose this morning?"

"Don't be silly and keep reading," she replied, not believing that to be the answer to the strange thing she'd witnessed earlier that day.

Fred continued. "Well it says she lives here in Brixham."

Chapter seven

With the aid of a map, Annie and Fred managed to find Eira Flynn's house. It was in the St Mary's area of the small fishing town.

"So how come you're on holiday with your aunt and not your parents?" Fred asked, looking through the heavy iron gates that barred their way to the building on the other side. "Haven't they got time for you or something?"

Annie pursed her lips. "They're dead," she replied. "They were killed in a boating accident when I was one. My aunt looks after me now."

There was a brief uneasy silence before Fred spoke. "I'm sorry."

"That's okay," she muttered, "you weren't to know."

"Yeah, but I should've been more thoughtful," he said. "I bet you really miss them?"

"A bit," she explained, looking down at her feet. "That's why I was a bit annoyed when you were a little rude to your mum. You don't know how lucky you are to have your parents still alive."

"What about your aunt?" Fred probed.

"Aunt Grace is really good to me; she treats me like I'm her own daughter," Annie pointed out. "Although I love her so much, I can't help but really miss my parents."

"I see," Fred said. "Do you think about them a lot?"

"All the time," Annie explained. "I dream about my mum every night. She'll sit on the end of my bed and chat to me before giving me a cuddle. The dreams are so vivid. When I'm asleep I see every detail of her flaming red hair and emerald green eyes. I also always remember her scent when I wake up; it's lavender."

"Do you dream about your dad as well?" Fred asked.

Annie shook her head. "No," she pointed out. "It's a bit strange, because I only ever dream about my mum and never about my dad. But I do think about him a lot in the day."

"Huh," Fred pondered. "I guess it's a good balance. You dream about your mum when you're asleep and think about your dad when you're awake."

Annie decided she didn't wish to continue the conversation – since talking about her parents made her cry – and pressed the intercom buzzer on the wall next to the gate.

It took several moments before it was answered. "Who's there?" a voice crackled through the small speaker.

Annie spoke into the intercom. "My name's Annabelle Short," she explained, using her full name to appear all proper. "I would like to speak to Eira Flynn about Thought People."

There was a short pause before the woman replied. "Go away!" her voice crackled through the speaker.

"Is that Miss Flynn?" Annie asked.

"Yes it is," the voice came through the speaker. "Now go away!"

"But it's important," she insisted. "I really need to speak to you."

The intercom buzzed to life again. "Go away! If you persist in harassing me I'll be forced to set the dogs loose on you and I've not fed them in a week."

Annie turned to Fred. "Any suggestions?"

The boy smiled. "Just one," he replied, walking up to the intercom.

He pressed down on the button and spoke. "Miss Flynn, I think I was attacked by a Thought Person this morning. I couldn't remember anything, but Annie told me she saw a shadow fly around my head until it disappeared into the trees."

There was a long wait, before all of a sudden the movement of machinery came from within the stone wall, which was quickly followed by the sound of tortured metal. The massive iron gates pulled themselves apart, creaking on their rusty old hinges.

Annie and Fred pushed their bikes through the gateway and over the gravel, which crunched under the wheels, towards the old building ahead.

Fred let out a long whistle. "This lady has a nice home."

"I think you're right," Annie replied, mesmerised by the large garden with a fountain in the middle. "It'd be great to jump in the fountain in this heat."

She then turned to the building in front. "It's beautiful," she whispered, looking at the giant windows and green vines that weaved up the walls to the roof.

"I know," he replied. "This is where I'm going to live when I've made my fortune from trading chocolate bars on the stock exchange."

The moment the pair reached the first step, the wooden door opened and an old woman emerged from within.

"Eira Flynn, at your service," she said.

"Hi, I'm Annie," Annie replied, looking at the small wiry woman sitting in an electric wheelchair. She had long snow white hair, wrinkles under her chocolate brown eyes and a soft smile. The woman's tiny frame made Annie think that the slightest gust of wind would blow her away.

"Pleased to meet you," Eira declared, moving her wheelchair towards the children. "Sorry about before, thought you were both just a pair of troublesome children."

"No, madam, we're not," Annie replied.

A smile crinkled across the old woman's weathered face. "So," she said, looking at Fred with interest in her eyes, "you had a run in with a Thought Person?"

Fred nodded, but Annie just shrugged – still not believing.

"Well, I guess the pair of you had better come inside," Eira said.

Chapter eight

The interior of the house was as magnificent as the exterior. The wooden floor, grand staircase with a stairlift running up the side, grandfather clock, paintings on the walls, suits of armour and antiques dotted about the place made it look like a stately house rather than an old scientist's home.

Eira led Annie and Fred into the main sitting room, where they sat on a large velvet chair in front of a massive window. Annie looked at the dust hanging in the air, illuminated by the sun's rays.

"So you had a run in with a Thought Person?" Eira questioned again, moving herself so she was opposite the children.

"I think so!" Fred gasped. "Annie said it flew around my head."

"That's very interesting," Eira pondered, running her fingers over the wrinkles on her forehead. "Very interesting indeed."

"So who are they?" Fred asked. "We want to know."

Eira looked up. "You get straight to the point, don't you?"

"Yes. We found your book, but the pages were torn out and the title had been scratched off," Fred blurted out again. "Who are they?"

"The question is, my boy, not who are they, but what are they?" the old lady declared.

"Huh?" the two children muttered together.

"You see, I've researched Thought People most of my life and what I've concluded is that they're not quite humans, but not quite ghosts. They're a little in between," Eira explained.

The old woman manoeuvred over to the mantelpiece, where she looked at a picture in one of the frames. It was one that showed her before she was confined to a wheelchair. "You see, Thought People are simply made up of human thoughts."

"Thoughts?" Annie asked.

"Yes! What I've discovered is that thoughts are like little sparks of electricity. Every time you think of something – be it remembering what you had for dinner last night to thinking about what you're going to do on the weekend – a small spark of electricity shoots around inside your head like a bolt of lightening," Eira explained. "But sometimes these sparks of electricity escape from your head."

"How?" Fred asked, transfixed.

"Simple, my boy," the old lady explained with a glint in her eye. "They escape through your nose of course."

Annie stood up. "That's rubbish!"

Eira grinned broadly. "Don't you believe me?"

"No!" Annie insisted. "The world revolves around science. It always has done and always will do."

"That's fine," she conceded. "Lots of people didn't believe me. They told me my theories were rubbish and I got laughed out of so many universities I've lost count. But I tell you I can prove it."

"How?" Annie asked.

"Easy," she answered. "By asking you a simple question. Have you ever forgotten something?"

"Err… of course," Annie replied, sitting back down.

"Something that you've tried really hard to remember?" Eira said. "Say, for example, you spent the whole of the weekend learning to spell several words in preparation for your spelling test on the Monday morning. You've learnt them so well that you know the words inside out and can spell them backwards whilst standing on your head. But the minute you get into the classroom you forget them. The thoughts have completely left your mind. Has that ever happened to you?"

"Err… yeah," she muttered.

"Ah-ha!" Eira cried, waving her finger in the air. "How could that happen? It's impossible. You spent the whole weekend learning the words off by heart until they were the only things that you could think about."

"Why did that happen then?" Annie asked.

"The answer, my girl," the old woman explained, "is that you didn't forget at all. Your thoughts shot out of your nose like a bolt of lightening."

There was a silence. *Could she be right?* Annie wondered.

Finally Eira continued. "These thoughts that have escaped are the seeds that create Thought People. You see, when enough thoughts escape from enough people the attraction becomes so great these bits of electricity will bind together in a flash of light that is accompanied by an ear-shattering bang!"

"And then what?" Fred whispered, now sitting on the edge of his seat.

"That's when a Thought Person is born – created by the discarded thoughts of a person," Eira said. "Forgotten thoughts of what a person watched on TV, what a child wanted for Christmas or even what they did on the weekend, they all go into making these unique creatures."

Annie didn't realise it, but she too was now sitting on the edge of her seat. "And then what happens?"

"I thought you didn't believe in them?" Eira asked with a smirk.

"I don't," Annie replied. "I'm just interested."

"Well if you're interested then I'll tell you that these beings live among us without us even knowing," Eira explained. "For them to survive they must constantly feed on people's discarded thoughts. Like we consume food in order to survive, they consume unwanted thoughts. If they don't feed on fresh thoughts they simply fade away into nothing."

"Well that's scary!" Fred gasped. "Stealing thoughts."

Eira laughed. "Don't be scared, my boy, there's nothing to worry about."

"If they live among us, then why have I never seen one?" Fred asked.

Eira smiled. "Are you sure you've never seen one?"

"Definitely!" he insisted.

"Oh, you've seen plenty of them, my boy," the old lady explained. "You just don't know it."

The two children looked puzzled.

"They could be anyone that you briefly meet," Eira said. "They could be the people standing behind you in the supermarket checkout queue, the young boy reading the football magazines in the newsagents or even the little old lady sitting on the back seat of the bus you're riding on.

"You may think they're normal humans, but in fact they're Thought People!" the old lady bellowed.

Annie stood up. "So they look like humans?"

"Of course," Eira replied, "they're made from discarded human thoughts and because of that they look like us."

Fred seemed worried. "That still scares me."

"There's nothing to be worried about," Eira explained, "they mean you no harm."

Annie still didn't fully believe that Thought People existed. "Okay, but what about the one that came out of Fred's nose?"

Hearing this new piece of information Eira's face turned to stone. It looked like she'd seen a ghost.

Chapter nine

Annie asked, "Are you okay?"

Eira swayed from side to side before slumping down in her wheelchair.

"Miss Flynn," Fred said, "are you okay?"

The scientist looked over to Annie, "Are you sure it came out of Fred's nose?"

Annie nodded. "I saw it with my own eyes, though I still don't believe it. Why?"

"Why?" Eira whispered. "This means that a terrible evil has returned."

Evil, Annie thought, her heart beating ever so slightly faster. *That's what the ghostly voice said. This is getting eerie.*

But she decided not to let her imagination run away with her. *How would Sir Isaac Newton deal with this?* she wondered, thinking about her hero from the world of science. He was a genius who hundreds of years earlier had thought up many of the scientific ideals that are used today. *He wouldn't think about ghosts, that's for sure. No, he'd find a rational reason for this. It's just a case of looking in the right place.*

"Evil?" she finally asked.

"Yes… evil," Eira said.

"Who?" Fred and Annie asked together.

"A horrible Thought Person who calls himself The Thought Stealer," the old lady muttered.

"Who's The Thought Stealer?" the pair asked.

"The Thought Stealer's horrible," Eira explained. "Just imagine all of the ghastly thoughts people have. I'm talking things like thinking about stealing a car, the urge to become a bully, the want to tell a lie or even the thought of cheating on a test. That's what he's made up of: utterly horrid thoughts."

"Can you tell us about him?" Annie asked.

The old lady began. "Well many years ago enough of these horrible thoughts escaped many people's heads and circled the world, meeting other bad thoughts. Negative thoughts attracted more negative thoughts and so on.

"The more bad thoughts that attracted each other, the bigger the mass of bad thoughts became, until one day there was an explosion of dark light!" the old lady explained.

"Then what happened?" Fred asked.

"The Thought Stealer and Vincent were born," Eira detailed. "Made of pure horrible thoughts and nothing else."

Stunned, Annie and Fred didn't speak and the room was so quiet you could hear a pin drop.

"They're pure evil," Eira muttered again.

"How do you know this?" Fred finally whispered.

"Because many years ago I battled with Vincent and he almost killed me. He was the one who put me in this wheelchair," she explained, tapping the wheels of her wheelchair with her bony old fingers.

"He was ghastly. But it wasn't Vincent that was inside you; it was his brother, The Thought Stealer."

"How do you know it was him?" Fred asked.

"Simple, my boy," Eira said. "He's not like a nice Thought Person, who will only feed on discarded thoughts. To prevent himself from fading away into nothingness, The Thought Stealer goes into a person's head through their nose and literally steals all of their thoughts."

"All of them?" Fred whispered, his hands trembling. "Wouldn't he only be interested in the bad thoughts?"

"You're right," Eira agreed. "But he steals all of the thoughts inside a person's head, before going off to a quiet place to feed on the horrible ones. Once he's finished he'll discard the rest."

This troubled Fred. "But why would he be inside my head? I don't have any horrible thoughts for him to feed on."

"Are you sure?" the old lady asked with a smirk.

Fred nodded.

Eira smiled. "Do you support a football team?"

"Huh?" Fred was puzzled.

"Well do you?" the lady demanded.

"Yeah, Liverpool," he explained.

"Ah-ha!" she bellowed, again waving a finger in the air. "Then I guess you don't like Manchester United?"

Fred was quick off the mark. "I hate them! I hope they get relegated. I –"

Before he finished the sentence about how he'd like to see the club closed down he stopped. His hatred for Manchester United was one of the things The Thought Stealer would have fed on.

The old lady was grinning. "Do you like eating vegetables?" she asked.

For a second time Fred was quick to reply. "No, I hate them! I –"

He again stopped mid-sentence.

Eira manoeuvred herself in front of the boy. "As you can see, there's something in all of us that The Thought Stealer can feed on."

Fred didn't argue and the old lady continued: "You were lucky that Annie got to you when she did. If he'd been left inside your head, he would have stolen everything until there was nothing left and that would have been the end of you. You would have spent the rest of your life as a mindless zombie."

The colour completely drained from Fred's cheeks.

"So how come he stopped when I arrived?" Annie asked. "And how come he didn't feed on my thoughts, instead telling me I'd been lucky, before threatening to feed on my thoughts later on?"

"You must have disturbed his feeding pattern," the old lady said. "Sometimes, if disturbed, he'll lose his concentration and won't be able to feed for an hour or so."

"Kind of like losing your appetite?" Fred suggested.

"Exactly!" Eira exclaimed.

"So why did you think it was The Thought Stealer, not his brother Vincent?" Annie asked.

The old lady looked over. "You see, Vincent had this idea of stealing so many thoughts that he would become more powerful than an army of monsters. And many years ago he came extremely close to achieving that."

"How?" Annie asked.

"He had a plan that entailed stealing the thoughts of all the people living in a village near here. If he'd succeeded, he would have consumed enough horrible thoughts that he would have never grown weak ever again," the old lady explained. "You see, if a nasty Thought Person consumes enough horrid thoughts in a short space of time, then they would achieve what I like to call a critical mass – eternal strength, where they would never become a shadow ever again and instead would become a very powerful being."

"So what happened?" Annie asked.

"When I got to Vincent he had consumed a lot of people's thoughts and was well on his way to achieving his critical mass. He had consumed enough bad thoughts that he would never fade away into a shadow, but he hadn't consumed enough to become all-powerful," the old lady remembered.

"I stopped him just in the nick of time," Eira sighed, shaking her head. "The battle with him got ugly and he almost killed me, because in an attempt to gain the critical mass he attacked me, trying to feed on my thoughts. Although I managed to stop him, I was left paralysed."

"Then what happened?" Fred asked.

"Vincent was defeated. He was prevented from becoming an incredibly powerful monster," Eira said. "After I defeated him, he was too weak to cause any more trouble. Now he's a feeble being, just like me."

"And what about his brother, The Thought Stealer?" Fred asked.

"He's obviously back to finish what his brother started. He wants to consume enough bad thoughts so that he can attain his critical mass and become a powerful monster," Eira explained, looking at the children who by now were mirroring her wide, frightened eyes.

Chapter ten

Eira moved over to the window. "I thought this day would never come. I thought that when I stopped Vincent, The Thought Stealer would be sensible and not try the same thing."

Annie looked at Fred. Both were as confused as each other. "What do we do now?" Fred whispered.

"I don't know, this still seems far-fetched," Annie mumbled, holding her hand over her mouth.

"How can you say that?" Fred whispered loudly. "From what you've seen and heard this morning, I can't believe that you still don't believe in things such as ghosts."

"Well I don't!" she snapped. "I don't believe in goblins, the Tooth Fairy, Santa Claus or even aliens."

"Aliens?" Fred gasped.

"Especially aliens," she snapped.

"Why not?" he asked. "What made you lose your hope that these brilliant things exist?"

Annie didn't answer, she just looked away.

Fred then turned to Eira, who was staring out of the window at some distant point.

"I should have destroyed The Thought Stealer," the old lady muttered to herself.

Annie stood up. Although she didn't believe in ghosts, maybe there was a more rational explanation for the existence of Thought People.

They're probably the result of a failed experiment by a mad scientist or something, she thought.

"So how do you destroy them?" Annie wondered.

Eira looked round. "I don't know, my girl. I thought I stopped all of this the first time round."

"And what did you do?" Fred asked, joining in on the conversation. "Can you tell us what happened when you met Vincent?"

"I was only young when I first encountered him. One day when walking my dog through the woods, I watched him appear out from amongst the trees and hang in the air as a big shadow." The old lady frowned.

"At first I was scared, but I quickly became intrigued and, without him seeing me, I spent the next few weeks studying him. He moved like a ghost, floating on the breeze, and fed on nasty children's thoughts. He would stalk the school bullies, knowing that he could get a good meal from their minds.

"As I watched his feeding patterns, I learnt that he wasn't just a primitive being. In fact he was intelligent, being able to read and write, and from some of the awful things I watched him do, I concluded he was pure evil," Eira explained.

She briefly stopped, to allow the children to digest what she was saying, before continuing. "I was stunned at what I learnt and told everyone I could find. But the thing was that no one believed me. I was just a kid who was telling a tale of a ghostly beast trying to steal thoughts. Because no one believed me, I took it upon myself to stop him."

"So what did you do?" Annie asked.

"I modified my father's vacuum cleaner, by fastening two straps to it so that I could wear it like a backpack," Eira detailed.

"With all of this ready, I hunted Vincent down and used the vacuum cleaner to drag him away from the people of the village for long enough so that most of them could escape, before he sucked their minds completely dry."

Annie brushed a loose strand of hair behind her ear. "So how do you suggest that we stop The Thought Stealer before he reaches the critical mass? Do you think the vacuum cleaner would work again?"

Eira shrugged her shoulders. "Possibly."

"Great!" Annie declared, looking over to Fred. "What do you think?"

Fred didn't answer.

"Hey, Fred, what do you think to that idea?" she enquired again.

Still Fred didn't answer. He just sat perfectly still, like a statue.

Suddenly Annie froze, because hanging in the air in front of the boy was a pulsating dark shadow with jagged edges. It was the same one that had come out of his nose earlier that day. It was The

Thought Stealer. And it looked like he'd got his appetite back.

Eira noticed this as well. "Good Lord, The Thought Stealer's come back to finish feeding on Fred's thoughts! He must have followed you both here!"

The horrible monster began to swoop around Fred's head, encircling him in darkness – preparing to fly up his nose.

"Fred, pinch your nose!" Annie yelled, remembering what the boy had read on the library computer database.

But Fred didn't answer. He just continued to sit there, transfixed, clearly too scared to move.

I need to save him! Annie's mind cried. *But how?*

The shadow transformed from a dark mass, with razor sharp edges, into a long line of murky matter. It was like a big dark spear.

With time running out, an idea quickly popped into Annie's mind. She darted over and tackled the young boy off his seat, right before The Thought Stealer flew up his nose.

The Thought Stealer missed his target and hit the seat at full force, knocking it over. But he didn't stay there for long, moving back into the air and circling the room in a dark cloud, readying himself to shoot up Fred's nose.

Still on the floor, Annie watched the wicked creature prepare to enter through Fred's nostrils. He swooped round, lined up and shot straight for the young boy.

Annie didn't have time to get out of the way, so she did the first thing that came to mind. She pinched Fred's and her own nose as tightly as she could.

It had the required effect, because The Thought Stealer stopped merely inches away from the boy's nose.

Fred's eyes then blinked open. "What are you doing?" he shrieked, despite his nose being blocked.

Annie was perfectly still. "Shhh, we've got a *broblem*," she whispered, unable to pronounce her *p*s owing to her fingers being pinched over her nose, blocking it.

The Thought Stealer turned from a spear-like shape back into the large mass of dark matter.

Seeing this, Eira grabbed hold of the fireplace, concerned about what was about to happen next.

"What's he doing?" Annie asked Eira, her heart now pounding away.

The old woman didn't reply. Instead she was wheezing heavily, as though suffering an asthma attack.

Aware Eira would be of little help, Annie watched The Thought Stealer begin to beat like a drum, causing the whole room to thud, bang and clatter!

The floorboards rattled, paintings dropped from the walls and the ornaments and pictures fell off the mantelpiece and smashed on the floor. It was as though they were being hit by an earthquake.

The shaking became more frantic and Annie and Fred were thrown about like laundry in the spin cycle of a washing machine.

Then the beast began to spin. His mass circled round the inside of the room, faster and faster. It felt like they were caught in the middle of a tornado.

As the wind whipped into a frenzy the two children clung together, right before they were swept off their feet by the furious storm and pulled into the air. But just before they were about to be spun wildly, Annie grabbed hold of the back of Eira's wheelchair. Fred clung to her with his free hand, holding his nose with the other.

Annie looked at the boy. "Whatever you do, don't let go of me or *bour* nose!"

Fred nodded frantically. "What do we do now?"

"We wait!" she yelled. "The Thought Stealer can't keep this up for long. I reckon he still hasn't fed so he'll grow tired very quickly!"

"But what if he's fed since you saw him last!" Fred shrieked, feeling his fingers begin to slip. The pair were being pulled into the centre of the room.

"Then we're in trouble!" the girl replied.

"Well hold on to the wheelchair!" Fred yelled.

"I'm trying!" she shouted back, her fingers sliding off the wheelchair. They were hanging in the air with only the heavy weight of Eira and her wheelchair stopping them from being pulled into the middle of the room, where The Thought Stealer would make mincemeat of them.

Annie looked around. The dark shadow that circled the room wasn't spinning as fast. *He's growing tired,* she thought.

But then the wind tugged so hard at her, she lost her grip on the wheelchair. And at that moment they were dragged into the middle of the room, where they were at the horrible monster's mercy!

Chapter eleven

Before The Thought Stealer overwhelmed them, something completely unexpected happened. The wind suddenly stopped and in the space of a second the room went still.

"I told you he'd grow tired," Annie smiled to Fred.

But Fred didn't mirror the girl's relief, because he knew there was one massive problem. They were now hanging in mid-air.

"Ah!" Annie and Fred cried, dropping through the air before hitting the floor with a *thud!*

Although her backside hurt from the fall, her eyes swiftly searched the room for the monster. It was an utter mess, far worse than her bedroom at home. The furniture was upside down, ornaments were smashed, paintings lay ripped and tattered and the rug that had been lying in front of the fireplace was now wrapped around the light hanging from the ceiling.

But The Thought Stealer was nowhere to be seen so she turned to Fred. "Keep *binching* your nose," she said, unable to pronounce her *p*s.

Fred rubbed the dust off his clothes and nodded.

Annie then turned to Eira. "Oh, no," she whispered, spying the old woman sitting slumped on the floor. Her wheelchair lay on its side.

She rushed over. "Are you okay?" she asked, helping the old lady back into her wheelchair.

Eira could barely force out a smile. "All that exertion's left me breathless and brought back my asthma," she wheezed.

"Where's your inhaler?" Annie asked, looking around.

"Don't worry about that," Eira gasped. "I'll be fine."

Annie then searched the room again for The Thought Stealer, but couldn't see him. "He's not here!" she declared.

"That doesn't matter," Eira breathed heavily. "He's in the house somewhere."

Annie looked at the old woman. "We'll run to the police station and get help. We'll try and get The Thought Stealer to follow us so that you'll be safe."

Eira didn't reply.

"Come on!" Fred urged. "We need to get out of here!"

Annie finally jumped up and, with Fred, charged out of the room and into the lobby. "Let's get our bikes and get to the police station as quickly as possible," she gasped, racing through the massive lobby towards the front door.

However, there was a problem! It was locked.

"What shall we do now!" Fred gasped.

"The windows!" the girl suggested. "We'll get out that way!"

Annie turned round, but stopped dead in her tracks. The Thought Stealer was hanging in the air in front of them. He suddenly transformed into a mouth.

"You two aren't going anywhere," The Thought Stealer rasped, his man-eating shark-like teeth menacing. "I'm going to enjoy stealing your thoughts."

"You can't! There's no way you can get inside our heads!" Annie spat, pinching her nose. Fred did the same.

"Oh, I don't think that'll be a problem," he growled, changing into a wicked smile.

Suddenly The Thought Stealer morphed back into the big dark shadow and then flew straight for a suit of armour. He oozed through the helmet and disappeared inside.

"I don't like the look of this," Fred muttered.

"I know what you mean," Annie responded, watching the silver metal suit jolt and jerk.

First the legs kicked out and then the arms. Seeming like an electric current was being passed through it, the suit of armour juddered violently.

The medieval body armour then stopped for several seconds before the helmet moved. Squeaking on its hinges, it turned round and looked directly at the children.

"We need to get out of here!" Fred gasped.

The suit of armour suddenly move like a real medieval knight was inside.

"Let's go in different directions!" Annie ordered, watching The Thought Stealer advance on them like a robot, with his sword above his head. "He can't chase the both of us at once."

"Good idea!" Fred cried, scuttling off towards the stairs.

Annie dashed off in the opposite direction. As she did though, she looked round and realised to her alarm that the monster had decided to follow her.

"This is just great," she muttered right before The Thought Stealer swung his sword in the direction of her head.

But as the brilliant blade sliced through the air she dived out of the way, falling hard on her knees. The sword clanged against the old rug that covered the stone floor.

Although her knees were throbbing she didn't bother to inspect her injuries, because the suit of armour was towering over her. The brute then raised his sword above his head a second time, and with a *swoosh!* brought it down like a hammer.

Even though Annie's reflexes were fast, rolling out of the way before her head was chopped clean off, the sharp blade caught a lock of her hair – severing it.

"That was close!" Annie gasped before looking up to see The Thought Stealer quickly lifting the blade above his head again and swinging it wildly.

Not giving the girl any time to breathe, he brought the weapon down in a flash of silver, as the sun's rays reflected off the blade's shiny surface.

Despite the fact that The Thought Stealer was intent on finishing Annie off, the young girl was speedy, rolling along the floor and avoiding the deadly weapon. The sword hit the floor with a *clang!*

In no time at all, the relentless monster had the sword back in the air and was quickly taking another strike.

But Annie was thinking super fast and this time she leapt for cover, right before the weapon hit the floor with another resounding *clang!*

Come on, Annie! her mind screamed. *You need to find away out of this!*

With her life in perilous danger, she swiftly looked from side to side. And that was when it hit her!

Just before The Thought Stealer could take another swipe, Annie slid through the gap between his legs and jumped to her feet. She darted off across the room.

Thinking that it was the most daring thing she'd ever done she quickly looked round, hoping to see the horrible Thought Person standing there all confused. The instant she did, however, her heart sank. "Oh give me a break," she groaned, seeing that The Thought Stealer was hot on her heels and raising his sword. He swung it in a dangerous arc!

Undeterred by the persistence of her foe, she hastily rolled forward, past the grandfather clock, and out of the path of the sharp blade, which embedded itself in the side of the wooden staircase with a *twang!*

Completing a perfect gym-class forward roll, Annie jumped to her feet before looking at The Thought Stealer. He was pulling the sword out of the wood.

"Great," she muttered, aware that she now had a couple of seconds of breathing time. She swiftly considered the limited options. *I can't run to the main sitting room, because in her weakened state Miss Flynn won't stand a chance against that brute,* she thought. *And I can't go up the stairs either,* noticing that The Thought Stealer was blocking that means of escape.

She was about to consider a third option, but realised she was out of time – The Thought Stealer had pulled the sword out of the side of the staircase. He raised it above his head and advanced on the young girl.

Breathing heavily, her cheeks rosy and thinking fast, Annie backed away from the dark creature as he readied for another attack.

In a life or death situation, crystal clear thinking is called for and Annie suddenly had a bright idea. With the blade cutting through the air, she grabbed the side of the grandfather clock and pulled with all her might, causing the large heavy time-piece to topple over.

Although it was quite spectacular, looking like a tree being felled by a lumberjack, The Thought

Stealer swung his sword with so much power he made light work of the clock. The metal blade smashed through the antique like a knife through butter, causing a thunderous explosion of wood, glass and metal cogs.

"It'll take more than that to stop me!" the shadowy creature snarled, preparing to finish the young girl off, who was now crouching on the floor having tried to protect herself from the flying debris.

"Can't anything stop this beast?" she gasped, turning round. But the moment she saw what was behind a chill ran down her spine.

To her horror she had backed into a corner. There was nowhere to run.

Knowing that the girl was trapped, The Thought Stealer smiled from behind the grille of the helmet as he advanced on her. He then raised the sword above his head for the final time. This swing would be fatal.

This is it! she thought, closing her eyes tightly shut. *I'm going to die!*

Chapter twelve

But before The Thought Stealer could bring the blade down, he was suddenly sent crashing across the room and onto the floor was an almighty *clatter!*

Having seen her life flash in front of her eyes, Annie wondered, "Am I dead?"

"Only dead lucky to be alive," Fred answered, whilst hanging from the chandelier in the middle of the lobby.

Annie's mouth fell open. "What are you doing up there?" she gasped.

"I ran up the stairs, climbed onto the banister and jumped across onto the chandelier," he explained. "I swung across and knocked him off his feet. Lucky I did; he was about to chop your head clean off."

"Thanks," Annie muttered, feeling her head to make sure that it was still there.

"Don't mention it," Fred replied, dropping off the chandelier and onto the floor. "Now let's wrap him up in this rug before he gets his strength back to fight us again."

"Good idea," Annie replied.

As the pair rolled up the rug, Annie asked, "I wonder why he wanted to kill us? I thought he was only after our thoughts?"

"I've no idea," Fred replied.

No sooner had the pair finished with The Thought Stealer than they found Eira. She was sitting slumped in her wheelchair in the corner of the main sitting room, with a clear oxygen mask over her face. It was attached to a bottle.

"What was all the commotion? I thought the pair of you were going to find the police?" she wheezed from behind the mask.

"We didn't need to," Annie declared with a smile. "We stopped that ghastly beast!"

"You stopped him!" Eira cried. "How?"

"We have him tightly rolled up in a rug!" Fred blurted out.

The old lady gasped, "That's great work!"

"So what do we do now?" Annie asked. "We still need to find out how he plans to be able to reach critical mass. Shall we interrogate him?"

Fred's grin returned. "Yeah, let's tickle him. The bullies at school always use that on me. It's horrible."

The group made their way into the lobby to where the suit of armour was lying rolled up tightly.

Eira manoeuvred around the carpet, collecting the sword lying on the floor as she did. "You definitely have him in there?" she breathed with difficulty, prodding the helmet with the sword.

"Sure have," Fred replied. "There's no way he could have escaped."

Eira's expression turned stern though, as she continued to poke the helmet.

"What's wrong?" Annie asked.

"The problem is, my girl, I think he's escaped," Eira said, forcing the helmet so that it detached from the rest of the suit and rolled onto the floor.

"Escaped!" Annie and Fred gasped together.

Eira leaned over and looked inside the suit of armour. "Empty, as I expected."

"I should have known," Annie groaned. "He simply floated out of the grille in the helmet to freedom. We should have blocked it."

Eira continued to wheeze. "He could be anywhere; we must be careful."

As the two children pinched their noses, Annie noticed that the old lady was still struggling to breathe. "Are you okay?" she asked.

"All the excitement has left me out of breath," the old lady gasped. "I need to get back to my oxygen mask."

Annie and Fred followed the old lady back into the main sitting room and helped her put on her mask.

"This place is making the hairs on the back of my neck stand on end," Annie muttered, studying every single shadow. The strong daytime sun made the shadow behind the door appear very sharp; the short shadows from the legs of the table seemed to move; and even the ones that Fred, Eira and herself cast along the floor looked menacing. Any one of them could be The Thought Stealer.

"Thanks for helping me," the old lady gasped, briefly removing her face mask.

"That's okay," Annie answered.

The young girl quickly examined the room for the horrible creature. Unable to find him, she looking back to Eira. "So now that he's failed to steal any thoughts, where would he have gone?"

The old lady's breathing remained laboured. "He would have gone back to his home."

"And where's that?" Annie wondered.

"It's somewhere nearby," she wheezed, "but I'm not sure where. All I know is that it's somewhere with a lot of shadows for him to melt into."

A place with lots of shadows, Annie pondered, failing to notice the dark matter in the old lady's face mask.

While taking deep laboured breaths, suddenly the old scientist's eyes went as wide as golf balls and her body froze.

"Miss Flynn!" Annie shrieked, noticing the old lady's stillness. "Miss Flynn!"

Eira didn't reply.

Then her body shook violently.

The children jumped out of the way as the old lady's body suddenly went out of control. It kicked, shook and jerked ahead of falling on the floor in a heap.

"What's going on?" Fred cried, thinking Eira looked like a toy being shaken by an angry child.

"It's The Thought Stealer!" she shouted back. "He must have got inside the oxygen tank!"

"We need to help her!" Fred cried.

However, they were too late because her body suddenly stopped moving and froze in a twisted jumble of arms and legs.

Several moments passed before Annie stared at Eira's face. There was a look of absolute terror in her eyes and her skin was as white as a sheet.

Then, taking the children by surprise, the shadow flowed out of the old woman's nose and into the air, where it amassed in the centre of the room in a big, floating, dark smear.

Whilst the children were standing, stunned, looking at the intimidating form, they pinched their noses extra tight.

The shape swiftly transformed into the mouth with pointed teeth that curled into a ghastly grin, before beginning to laugh. It was so loud it cut through the air like a knife. "Ha, ha, ha, ha, ha!"

"Annie!" Fred screamed at the top of his voice. "Make him stop!"

"I can't!" she yelled, watching the windows shatter and explode everywhere.

Shielding her face from the flying glass with her arms, Annie thought her eardrums would burst!

Then all of a sudden it stopped and the dark form disappeared out of the room.

Chapter thirteen

The twosome just stood in the middle of the mess that covered almost every bit of the room, staring at Eira. She was lying on the floor as rigid as a rock, looking as though she'd been scared stiff.

Annie's shock quickly wore off though. "Miss Flynn!" she yelled, rushing over to the old woman. "Wake up!"

There was no response. She continued to rest on the floor like a statue that had been knocked over.

Annie put her mouth to the scientist's ear. "Miss Flynn, wake up!"

Fred joined in. "Miss Flynn! Snap out of it!" he yelled, clicking his fingers in front of the old lady's nose.

Again the woman didn't move.

Annie then commented, "She looks alive."

"Well what's wrong with her?" he asked.

She mumbled, "The Thought Stealer's fed on her thoughts. Her head must have been sucked dry and there's nothing left inside."

"This is horrid!" Fred gasped. "She's alive, but she has no thoughts inside her brain."

Annie stood up. "It's like the lights are on, but there's no one home."

"What shall we do now?" Fred asked. "What about science? I thought you said it had all the answers. Does it have the answer to this?"

Can science help Miss Flynn? she wondered, scratching the back of her head, trying to remember everything she'd learnt at junior science club.

"Sir Isaac Newton would know what to do," she muttered, looking down at Eira.

"Sir Isaac who?" Fred cut in.

"My hero, Sir Isaac Newton," Annie explained. "Although he's been dead for well over two hundred years, he's the great scientist who discovered gravity after an apple fell out of a tree and hit him on the head. His findings are still used in science today."

Fred was interested. "Like what?"

Annie knelt down and prodded the old lady's arm. But there was no reaction. She then looked up to Fred. "Have you ever heard of the saying 'for every action there is an equal and opposite reaction'?"

Fred nodded. "Yeah, but I'm unsure about what it means though."

"Well, he came up with that," she explained. "He discovered that everything has an opposite. Simply put, like when there's day there's night, when there's up there's down and when there are boys there are girls."

"And when there's someone who's sceptical about ghosts, like you, there's someone who believes, like me," Fred added.

Annie smirked at the boy's smart comment. "Very funny."

"Well how's this going to help Miss Flynn?" Fred asked.

"I'm not sure," Annie mumbled.

"A great help this Sir Isaac what-do-you-call-him is," Fred muttered. "Maybe science doesn't have the answers after all."

"Yes it does!" Annie fired back. "We're just not looking in the right place."

"Well where's the right place?" Fred quizzed.

Annie didn't know. What she needed was a *Eureka!* moment. Just like when an apple fell on Sir Isaac Newton's head. Back then it had sparked him into thinking about what caused things to fall to earth. She needed something that would spark her mind into thinking about what would help Eira and stop The Thought Stealer once and for all.

Finally she concluded she wasn't going to find the answer in Eira's sitting room. She needed to look elsewhere. And that was when a thought popped into her mind. "If we're going to help her, we need to find The Thought Stealer."

"Are you crazy?" Fred shrieked. "He's too dangerous!"

"Look!" she insisted. "It's about time he became the hunted, instead of the hunter. And besides, I've got an idea that might just work."

Chapter fourteen

Having phoned for an ambulance, the pair decided to leave Eira's house before it arrived. Annie figured that explaining to the paramedics that the old woman's thoughts had been stolen seemed too far-fetched and for that reason a quick exit was the best option.

Annie decided though that if they didn't manage to find a way of helping her, they'd visit her in hospital later that day to see if her condition had improved.

Having phoned her aunt to let her know that she and Fred were okay, Annie turned to the boy and asked, "Now you don't mind continuing to help me?"

"It's fine," Fred insisted. "Why?"

"I just feel a bit guilty about keeping you away from your friends. It's just gone lunchtime and you probably have plans to go for a bike ride or something," Annie said.

"It's fine," Fred repeated. "Like I said, I didn't really have any plans."

"Okay," Annie said, wondering why Fred didn't have any plans on such a beautiful day. If she lived in Brixham, every day of her summer holiday would have been taken up by either going to the beach with her aunt or taking a boat trip.

"But there's just one thing I'd like to ask," Fred enquired, feeling the cold chill of the air-conditioner on his arms and legs. "Explain to me why we're back at the library?"

"It's simple," Annie replied, leading Fred towards the computer terminals. "If we're going to find out where The Thought Stealer lives, then we just need to look in the right place."

"And where is the right place?" he asked.

A small smile appeared across her lips. "That beast steals all of a person's thoughts in order to feed on the bad ones to prevent himself from fading away, before discarding the thoughts he doesn't need, right?"

"Okay," Fred replied, puzzled.

"You would consider that weird, wouldn't you?" she asked.

"I guess so," he mumbled.

"Well weird things get written about," she explained, sitting down in front of one of the computers and pulling Fred into the seat opposite. "You know, in ghost stories and such."

Suddenly Fred's blue eyes brightened. "You think that the monster's thought stealing has been documented somewhere as an odd and unexplained event?"

"Exactly!" she whispered loudly, trying not to disturb the people sitting reading quietly. "Now all we need to do is look through back dated issues of the local newspaper for stories about strange things happening in and around Brixham."

"Won't that take all afternoon?" Fred asked.

"Not if you know what you're looking for," she said. "Copies of the local newspaper, the *Herald Express* I think, I'm sure have been archived in the reference section of the computers. And you being a computer whiz it will take you no time at all to find something of interest."

"I like it!" Fred exclaimed with a grin.

He swiftly positioned himself in front of the computer, pushing Annie out of the way in the process, and quickly started to type away at the keyboard.

In no time at all he found the archived editions on the computer's database and began to search. He used keywords such as *unexplained events* and *ghostly happenings.*

But after half an hour, nothing of interest had come up.

"Maybe we're looking for the wrong thing?" Fred suggested.

Annie just frowned, her frustration evident.

"I'm just making a suggestion," he said, holding up his hands.

She stood up and paced back and forth. "Try the keywords *hideous shadow*," she suggested.

Fred nodded and typed the keywords *hideous shadow* into the computer.

He waited several moments before looking over to the girl. "Nope, that's not any good."

"Okay, try *evil monster*," Annie suggested.

Fred typed the words into the computer. But again it didn't generate anything of interest.

Annie was becoming more frustrated. "What would the effects of The Thought Stealer's thought stealing be? Because that's what someone would write about," she pondered out loud.

"Well after he consumes someone's thoughts, they're left like statues with their eyes wide open," Fred suggested.

"That's it!" she cried.

"Shhh," a person sitting reading a book in the corner demanded.

"Sorry," Annie replied, before turning her attention to the boy. "Type in the keyword *zombie*."

"Zombie?" Fred asked

"Yeah!" she whispered loudly. "I bet people have been found like zombies after the shadowy beast has stolen all their thoughts and I reckon a journalist has written about it."

Fred typed the word *zombie* into the computer and in no time at all the results came up on the screen.

Annie looked at the results and clicked on one that caught her interest. It read: *A zombie found in Brixham.*

She read the article, which was over ten years old. "Today, a person has been found in a trance-like state. The man, between twenty and thirty years of age, was found by a woman walking her dog on Grey Pebble Cove. His eyes were wide open and his body was rigid, like a statue."

Annie scratched her chin before continuing. "Although the man was taken to hospital for an examination and the doctors concluded he was healthy, they could find no activity inside his head. One doctor said it was as though his mind had been sucked out."

"What do you reckon?" Fred asked.

"Sounds like The Thought Stealer has been pretty busy," she muttered.

"You're telling me," Fred replied, before looking for another article that might be of interest.

But after several minutes of searching, nothing of interest came up. "So what now?" he asked.

"I think I might have an idea," she muttered, jumping out of her seat and dashing over to the *Local studies* section. She was looking for a book that referred to Grey Pebble Cove.

Her eyes scanned the many books until she found the one she was interested in. It was titled *Coves and Beaches of South Devon.*

As she pulled it off the shelf Fred joined her. "What're you looking for?" he asked.

"One second," Annie insisted, flicking to the index at the back of the book.

She searched through the index until she found the reference to Grey Pebble Cove. It was on page forty-nine.

The girl quickly flicked to the page and after several minutes of reading the contents she spoke. "Here we go," she said to Fred, pointing at a passage of interest.

Fred peered over and read it out loud. "Grey Pebble Cove is the oddest of all of Devon's coves. Not only does the place have the highest level of reported paranormal activity, but people have gone to the place and never returned. It is the place that all of the local children believe is haunted by the shadow creatures."

He then turned to Annie. "The Thought Stealer?"

Annie smiled. "Exactly," she replied, with a glint in her eye. "If the reporter who'd written the article had bothered to do a little research, he would have discovered that what had happened to that man wasn't a one-off incident."

Annie continued. "I think this is where The Thought Stealer lives and feeds. I reckon he waits in the shadows for unsuspecting victims to walk by before he pounces."

"Sounds pretty convincing," Fred replied, walking back to the computer with Annie. "Where's the cove?"

Annie reread the news article until her eyes found a small map. It showed where the victim had been discovered. "I think we should take a ride out there," she suggested. "If we find The Thought Stealer's hideout, then we might be able to discover something to stop him from reaching critical mass.

We may also be able to find something that could help return Miss Flynn's thoughts."

"Do you think that's wise?" he groaned. "Considering the fact that people have gone in there and come out with their minds sucked dry – that's if they come out at all?"

"Don't be such a baby," she baited, rising from her chair. "Or do you want everyone to know you're a bigger wimp than a girl?"

Chapter fifteen

"So why are you so obsessed with science?" Fred asked, negotiating his bike down the tricky path leading to Grey Pebble Cove. "I mean it's not exactly the type of thing I'd expect a ten-year-old girl to be interested in."

Annie slowed her bike so she was riding alongside the boy. "I just think science makes sense. It explains why the sun comes up in the morning, why things fall to earth, why it rains and why there are stars in the sky. It provides all the answers," she explained, weaving her bike round the large stones on the path.

"Okay, but why don't you believe in ghosts?" he asked.

"I just don't!" she snapped. "It's such a stupid thing to believe in."

"But, Annie," Fred urged. "For me, believing in ghosts is what makes a kid a kid. What happened to you to make you stop believing?"

This time Annie didn't answer. Her reason for not believing was something that Fred would never understand. Before Fred could probe further, she set her sights on the small dark cove ahead and rode off down the path. The boy put his bike into a higher gear and gave chase.

The cove was dark, the sun's rays blocked out by the trees above, and Annie couldn't see a single soul about. All she could see was millions of small pebbles covering every inch of the cove in a sea of grey and black dots.

It was so dark, the water that lapped against the shore looked like treacle.

"This place gives me the creeps. How can the cove be so dark, whereas the rest of the bay is being bathed in the early afternoon sunlight?" Fred whispered, looking out across the blue water and clear sky. He noticed that, other than a small tall ship anchored off the shore, there were no vessels in the water. It was eerily quiet.

"The trees from the woods seem to be blocking out most of the light, but that doesn't explain why it's so dark," Annie thought out loud. She then turned her attention to an old building standing on the rocks in the corner of the cove. It looked like a small tower that had suffered centuries of being battered by all that the sea and weather could throw at it.

"Well whatever's causing this place to be so dark, it's perfect for The Thought Stealer. There are shadows everywhere. He could be happily hiding in any one of them," Fred noticed. "What's the plan?"

"We check out the building in the corner," she answered.

As the children rode over to the edifice, the more its neglect was apparent. The stone was crumbling to dust and it was on the verge of collapsing. Annie wondered why it was there. *Was it an old lookout from a forgotten battle?* she thought.

She jumped off her bike, hobbled across the stones and climbed up the small rock face to where the little tower was standing. Once at its base she looked round. "Fred, come up!"

Fred wasn't too sure, but climbed up anyway.

She then turned to the small tower and peered through the hole in the wall where the door once stood. Finally she tentatively stepped inside, but what she found left her disappointed. There was nothing but four stone walls and a square hole in the ground, with a rusty ladder leading down into the darkness.

Fred followed her in and looked down the hole. "So what do you think's down there?"

Annie gave him a mischievous smile, before racing back to the bikes. When she returned, she was armed with the bikes' headlamps.

"I'm going down to take a look," she explained, switching on the powerful light and clipping it to her T-shirt. She handed the other light to Fred before climbing down the first couple of rungs. "You coming?"

Again Fred was cautious. "I don't know – it might be dangerous. Why do we have to go down there anyway?"

"If we're to find out how to help Eira and prevent The Thought Stealer from carrying out whatever dastardly plan he has in mind, then we have no choice but to investigate," Annie explained.

Fred still wasn't so sure.

"Come on, Fred," she called up, descending the ladder. "Other than that horrible shadowy monster, what do you think's down there, a ghost or something?"

"Possibly," he whispered, giving in to Annie's demands. He started to climb down the ladder.

No sooner had the twosome disappeared into the dark void below than the water rats that had been hiding in the rocks around the cove scuttled into the tower and disappeared down the hole in pursuit.

But these rats weren't small cuddly rodents – they were very big beasts indeed.

Chapter sixteen

"Are you scared?" Fred asked, descending the ladder.

"No!" she whispered loudly. "As I keep telling you, I don't believe in ghosts and so long as we keep our fingers over our noses if we see The Thought Stealer, then we should be okay."

"Well if you're not scared of The Thought Stealer and you don't believe in ghosts, then why are you whispering?" he asked with a smug grin.

"I'm not whispering because I'm scared of ghosts or The Thought Stealer, I'm whispering because there might be bats down here."

"Bats!" Fred cried.

"Shhh," Annie put her finger to her lips, "you don't want to make too much noise as they have sensitive ears and you might wake them."

Suddenly Fred looked up. "Did you hear something?"

"Hear what?" Annie asked.

"I'm not sure," he whispered, listening. "It sounds like a kind of scratching."

Annie stopped and listened. "I can't hear anything."

"Let me have a look," Fred said, unclipping his flashlight off his T-shirt and pointing it upwards. But what he saw was terrifying. "Annie, try and get down the ladder as fast as you can!"

"Why?" she asked.

"Because there are huge rats crawling down the wall after us!" he shrieked.

Annie pointed her light upwards and saw the massive beasts crawling down the wall, using the imperfections in the stone for footholds. Not wanting to be eaten alive, she quickly descended the ladder.

The moment she was on the ground the cold air stabbed at her cheeks, turning them red. She then waved her flashlight around and noticed she was standing in a small passageway, cut into the rock.

Fred soon joined her. "This isn't good," he frowned, spying the first rat that appeared at the bottom.

"It's horrible," she whispered, looking at the large rodent with a pointy nose, beady black eyes and long tail. Its hairy coat was wet, making it look like it'd been dipped in a barrel of oil. Another rat then appeared and raised its nose into the air.

"I've never seen rats that big!" Annie whispered loudly.

"I bet they were bred by The Thought Stealer," Fred suggested. "He probably trained them to protect whatever's down here."

As several more rats appeared at the bottom, Annie's heart quickened; they were bigger and uglier than the others.

"This isn't good," she muttered, watching several more rats appear at the bottom. Her eyes then moved to the rodent that stood out. With its grey coat and beady red eyes she knew it was the head rat!

She then turned to Fred. "I suggest we make a run for it."

"I'm not going to disagree with you!" he cried, grabbing the girl's hand before dragging her down the passageway.

The moment they moved, the rats acted. The rodents darted off in pursuit of the two children.

"What now?" Fred yelled.

"Just keep running!" she replied, looking at the stone walls. They were slimy and water was dripping from the stalactites hanging from the ceiling onto the floor. "Be careful, the floor's slippery."

Fred nodded.

Annie's heart was pounding, not knowing where she was going or what was at the end of the passageway.

Fred looked behind. "They're gaining!" he yelled, spying the army of rats scurrying up behind them. The grey rat was leading; his eyes burning like fire and his teeth looking as sharp as knives.

Annie didn't look round, since she was more concerned about the T-junction ahead. The passageway went left and right.

Although she didn't know which way to go, when she looked round she knew she'd have to think fast! The grey rat was almost behind them, ready to sink its teeth and claws into her.

She decided to go left.

The water rats followed, and were about to attack when Annie suddenly stopped.

Fred crashed into her and the pair fell on the floor. But her sudden stopping had the desired effect. The rat's claws had no grip on the slimy floor. They tried to stop, but continued by, sliding like they were on ice. The rodents lost all control and piled into each other in a massive heap.

Annie was quick to react, jumping to her feet, grabbing Fred and racing off down the right-hand passageway.

"That was a good move!" Fred panted, shining his light on the rats. They were fighting with each other, trying to get up.

"Thanks," Annie gasped, racing down the passageway before coming to a large wooden door.

Annie inspected it and quickly noticed the doorknob was rusted tight.

"Get the door open!" Fred yelled, looking at the rats, which had now reorganised themselves and were back in hot pursuit.

"I'm trying to!" she replied, rattling the doorknob.

"Well try faster!" Fred shrieked; the rats almost on them, ready to pounce.

In frustration, Annie quickly stepped back and booted the door knob with her trainer. With a *screech* of tortured metal, it gave way.

"Yes!" Annie cried, pulling the door open. She grabbed Fred and pulled him through the doorway before slamming it shut. The rats banged into the door with a muffled *thud!*

"Well that was close," she muttered, shining her light around.

The beam cut through the darkness and cast a spot on the wall. But what she saw made her jump. Because on the wall was the carving of a human face etched into the stone. But this face was grotesque, like a gargoyle. Its features were trapped in a state of absolute terror: mouth open, gasping, and eyes staring, terrified.

"This is horrid," she whispered, moving the light around the room.

There were more and more faces carved into the stone. All different, but all had pained expressions and they all looked like they were trying to escape from the rock face.

"Who would have carved such ghastly things?" Fred asked, looking at the faces.

"I'm not sure," she replied, before spying a faint glimmer of light emanating from a passageway at the end of the room. "Hey, Fred, come over here."

As the pair made their way down the dark passageway, towards the light at the end, Annie became aware that the walls were similar to the ones in the cave they had just left. Tortured and pained faces were cut into the stone, seemingly trying to escape.

Annie attempted to stop herself from looking at them, instead trying to keep her eyes on the light. It was coming from the other side of the wooden door at the end.

As soon as she got to the door, she switched her light off and peered round. Fred joined her, switching his light off too.

What was behind was very worrying though. Inside the cave, which was lit by burning torches hanging from the walls, were three figures draped in dark red cloaks. They had hoods over their heads, disguising their faces. On the floor around the figures were small yellow crystals.

Some of the crystals were jagged and dull, whereas others were shiny like glass, twinkling in the shimmering light. In the middle was a large yellow crystal that was almost half Annie's size.

"What are they doing?" Fred whispered.

"I've no idea," Annie replied, watching the figures arrange themselves in a circle.

Then, out of the darkness above, a shadow floated down and hung in the air just above the ground. With its sharp edges, Annie recognised it immediately; it was The Thought Stealer.

The shadowy beast floated in the air for several moments, before morphing into the shape of a human and lowering himself onto the floor.

The three cloaked figures dropped to their knees and pulled their hoods back.

Annie let out a gasp, spying what was beneath. Instead of human heads, there were head-shaped shadows. *They're just like The Thought Stealer,* she thought. *They must also be made of horrible thoughts.*

"Very good," the dark monster rasped to the figures, examining the massive crystal. "You have done well to find this crystal. The small crystals are useless to me, but this big one is perfect."

The figures nodded.

"His voice is horrible," Fred whispered. "It's almost as horrible as nails being scraped across a blackboard."

"I know what you mean," Annie replied, before listening further to what The Thought Stealer had to say.

"I want you to move this big crystal to our secret hideout near to where I will attack tonight," The Thought Stealer ordered.

"Yes, master," the cloaked figures replied obediently.

"Be very careful," The Thought Stealer said.

The figures nodded in obedience.

"He's planning an attack tonight?" Annie whispered, her heart pounding. "But where and why?"

She turned to Fred. "I don't think we're going to find anything here that's going to help Miss Flynn. We have to change our plan. We need to get back and warn someone about the attack."

Fred nodded and they quietly tiptoed away from the room and down the passageway. But that was where they realised they were in deep trouble. Because hanging from the ceiling in front were hundreds of bats.

Chapter seventeen

Their bodies were hanging upside down, wrapped in their black wings, and they were like the water rats – large and creepy.

"Don't move a muscle," she whispered, grabbing Fred's arm. "As I said, they're sensitive to sound and vibrations. If we're quiet enough, they might not even know we're here."

Fred nodded and the pair slowly moved through the passageway.

Annie kicked herself for not noticing them before. She had been so concerned with the light behind the door she hadn't bothered to look up at the ceiling. If she had, she would have seen them. She then wondered, *Has The Thought Stealer also trained them to protect these caves?*

Annie held Fred's hand and felt how sweaty it was. He was scared, so she gave him a smile.

But the moment Fred smiled back was the moment he took his eyes off the ground. In the space of a heart stopping second, he lost his footing, slipped on the slimy floor and crashed flat on his face.

As Annie looked up at the bats, the hairs on the back of her neck stood on end. "This isn't good," she muttered, watching the small mammals awaken. Their ears pricked up like antennas and their heads turned to face the two children.

Annie grabbed Fred and pulled him to his feet. "We better make a run for it," she whispered.

Fred didn't argue and the two children charged off.

Running for their lives, she looked up. All of the bats were now conscious of their presence. They all spread their dark, Count Dracula, cape-like wings and dropped from the ceiling. In no time at all the air was filled with giant bats; their wings flapping, ears pricked and sharp teeth exposed.

They flew after the two children.

Annie looked to Fred. "Keep running!" she shrieked, deciding there was no more need to be quiet.

"But what about the rats?" Fred cried back.

A shiver ran down her spine. "We're trapped!" she yelled, remembering that the rats were in the passageway leading to the ladder.

They were being chased by a hundred hideous bats, towards an army of huge, hungry water rats.

Annie looked round. One of the bats swooped down, its teeth ready to sink into her neck. She ducked out of the way and it flew by before crashing into the wall. Several more bats circled, their wings hitting the children's heads.

"Annie!" Fred yelled, fighting off the mammals. "This is horrible!"

"I know!" she replied. "Just keep your hands over your head and continue running!"

"But what about the rats; they'll be waiting for us!" he shouted.

"We'll deal with that when we get to it!" she cried.

The pair fought with the bats, while running for the door at the end. Every time the bats attacked, the children ducked out of the way, or fended them off with their lights.

Being swamped by the bats, they got to the door. Annie booted it open and the pair dived through.

However, what greeted them was horrid.

The rats sat obediently – the grey one at the front – at the heels of their master who loomed over Annie, his dark form imposing.

"The pair of you are becoming quite troublesome," The Thought Stealer hissed.

Chapter eighteen

Annie and Fred were carried by the bats back into the cave containing the yellow crystals, followed by The Thought Stealer, his goons and the rats. Hanging in the air by the bats' claws, the two children pinched their noses.

"As you have no doubt guessed, I have trained these rats and bats to protect me and my cave," The Thought Stealer explained. "I nurtured them from birth and fed them chemical waste. You see, the waste has a funny effect on them, since it makes them grow more than five times their original size."

Annie didn't answer. She just looked at The Thought Stealer, who now appeared like a human-shaped shadow. His pointy nose, crooked teeth and narrow red eyes, sunk into his head, were hideous. In fact there wasn't a single pleasant thing about the form that was made of nothing more than nasty thoughts.

Annie then looked over to the three figures, who had now placed their hoods back over their heads, so all she could see was a dark void underneath.

"Did you come here to try and stop me?" The Thought Stealer asked, examining the children like a bully looking at a bug he wished to pull the legs off.

"Yes!" Annie spat.

He laughed. "You're not going to stop me. No one can. All of the other Thought People tried to stop me, but I was too strong for them and I ended up imprisoning them in the walls of these caves," he hissed, the features on his face turning into a horrible smile. "Like scavengers, they now feed off the thoughts I discard."

Annie was revolted. The nicer Thought People were trapped in an eternal state of pain and misery.

The horrible monster added, "You don't even know what I plan to do."

"Well why don't you tell us," Fred demanded.

The Thought Stealer continued to laugh. "Oh I won't be doing that. Only in rubbish movies does the bad guy outline his dastardly plan to the good guys. All you need to know is that tonight your little town will succumb to me, as I steal all of their thoughts."

"Why?" she asked. "Do you plan to achieve a critical mass?"

The Thought Stealer didn't answer. Instead he suddenly transformed from the human shape into the black cloud. He then floated into the air and joined all of the bats, which were seemingly waiting for their master to give them instructions.

He glided over, so that he was close to Annie's nose. She felt the cold air that encircled his whole form. It looked like steam was coming from her mouth, but from junior science club she knew that the cold air caused the water vapour in her breath to cool down and turn into a watery form. It was called condensation.

"What am I going to do with the pair of you?" he quizzed, circling them like a lion round its prey.

"I bet you're going to consume our thoughts?" Fred pointed out the obvious. "Just like you tried to do this morning?"

"Oh, I don't think I'm going to feed on *your* thoughts," The Thought Stealer rasped.

The shadowy creature then floated close to Annie's face. "No, maybe I'll eat yours," he taunted, licking the lips that had formed in the middle of the dark cloud.

Annie pinched her nose tightly. Fred did the same.

The Thought Stealer then turned to the three cloaked figures. "As a reward for your good work, you may have the bad thoughts inside these children's minds. Just discard the rest."

"Thank you, master," the three figures muttered together, right before The Thought Stealer disappeared out of the cave.

The children were lost for words, as the bats took them out of the cave and down the passageway. They struggled frantically, trying to break away from the bats' grip. But it was no use; they were far too strong.

"Annie, what do we do now?" Fred asked, trying to break free.

"I'm working on it," she replied, looking down at the cloaked figures following behind. They looked like hungry animals waiting in anticipation of a good feed.

The children were swiftly taken into another cave, which was lit by burning torches and had all of its walls covered by tortured faces. She looked around and noticed a small stream running along the ground. It disappeared into a hole in the wall. She remembered from school that very often streams ran underground through rock formations, before appearing out in the open many miles away.

Suddenly they were dropped on the floor and one of the cloaked figures clicked his fingers, causing several more bats to fly into the room like a plague and dive straight for Fred.

The young boy swiped with his free hand, his other pinching his nose, fending the creatures off.

Seeing this Annie joined in and grabbed one of the bats by the leg and pulled it out of the air. She then swung it around her head and threw it at the wall. The creature hit the wall with a *splat* and slid down onto the ground completely dazed.

"Keep *bour* fingers pinched over *bour* nose!" Annie yelled, pronouncing *y* as a *b* owing to her nose being blocked.

She went for another bat.

But this time the creature was aware of what she was trying to do. It clearly didn't want to suffer the same fate as its companion, so it hovered out of the way of her flailing hands.

Fred continued to fight with the creature that pecked and gouged at him. He dropped his light in the process. Annie grabbed the beast by the legs and attempted to pull it away from the boy. But the moment she did, another bat swooped down, grabbed her by the foot and picked her up.

Annie was lifted and in no time was hanging upside down. She fought with the bat, trying to get it to release its grip. But it was no use, and the creature easily carried her into the centre of the cave. She swung frantically with her light, trying to smash the monster out of the air.

Fred kept his fingers pinched tightly over his nose, and at the same time fought with the horrible beast. But as a second bat joined in, the boy was forced to fight it off with the hand that was holding his nose.

Hanging upside down, Annie saw this. "Fred, keep *bour* fingers pinched over *bour* nose!" she yelled.

"I'm trying!" he cried back, wrestling with the bats.

Annie turned her attention to The Thought Stealer's goons, who had been waiting for one of the children to let go of their nose. Seeing that Fred's nostrils were exposed, the three figures suddenly oozed out of their cloaks and floated into the air. They looked just like The Thought Stealer: dark clouds of bad thoughts.

Annie watched, helpless, as the three ghastly beasts flew into the air and swirled around the cave. Fred continued to fight with the two giant bats, while the three dark clouds lined up and shot straight for his nose.

"No!" Annie screamed, watching the dark shadows fly up the boy's nostrils.

The moment they entered his head, just like what had happened earlier in the day, the young boy went like a statue. He stopped fighting with the bats and his eyes glazed over.

Chapter nineteen

Whilst hanging upside down, Annie's mind cried, *I need to help him!*

She looked up at the bat, which she was dangling from, and instantly noticed it wasn't paying attention to her. Instead it was watching Fred's mind being consumed. Thinking fast, she quickly took advantage of this by swinging her light and smashing it into the creature's body, causing it to *squeal!*

Shocked, the bat dropped her and she hit the ground with a bump.

With her elbows hurting from the fall, she looked over at Fred. He remained standing still. Her eyes then moved to the two bats which were both hovering, watching the boy.

Annie rushed up behind one of the creatures, and taking it by surprise, grabbed it by its claws and pulled it out of the air. Startled, the creature screamed and flapped its wings. But Annie was undeterred, spinning it round and propelling it at the other bat.

It smashed into its horrible companion and together they fell onto the ground in a pile.

Annie didn't hang around. "You're not going to steal my friend's thoughts!" she yelled, charging over to the boy she was growing to like and shaking his shoulders.

"Fred!" she cried. "Snap out of it!"

But Fred continued to stare vacantly.

"Fred!" she cried again, shaking him more vigorously. "Don't let them eat your thoughts!"

Still Fred remained like a statue.

Annie's own mind was running at lightening speed. *If I can't snap him out of the trance, then I'll have to try something else.*

She looked round the cave for something to use. But there was nothing. All that seemed to cover every inch of the space was slime.

Remaining undeterred, Annie continued to search. Her eyes looked everywhere, before a thought popped into her mind. Quickly she put her light into her back pocket before reaching into her front pockets, where she felt the grains of sand that had been in there since the previous day.

In an instant, she grabbed a handful of sand, ran up to Fred and sprinkled it around his nose and over his head.

The haze swirled around his face for several moments, but nothing happened.

"Come on!" she urged, scooping up another handful from her pocket and rubbing it under his nose.

Annie was about to grab a third handful of sand when Fred's nose twitched. It was ever so slight to start with, but then it twitched again.

Suddenly he sneezed. "Achoo!"

"Great!" she cried, picking out the last of the sand from her pockets and rubbing it under his nose.

"Achoo!" He sneezed again.

Annie watched Fred continue to sneeze. It was frantic and rapid. Every time he sneezed a cloud of dust came out of his nose that was followed by a small bit of dark matter.

"That's good!" she urged. "Keep sneezing!"

In no time at all Fred sneezed the horrible Thought People out through his nostrils and into the air.

She then looked over to the boy, who was blinking. "Hey there," she smiled, "how you feeling?"

"What just happened?" Fred muttered, looking around. "Did I just have another nasty Thought Person inside my head?"

Annie nodded. "You had three," she explained, pointing to the three dark blobs floating in the air, confused.

"Three of them?" Fred shrieked. "This is –"

Before he could finish his sentence, Annie cut in. "Come on, let's go!" she urged, pulling her light from her pocket and dragging him into the passageway.

But that was where the pair stopped. Because standing in their way were the water rats that had been guarding the door. The grey rat's red eyes glared and its mouth curled back, exposing its sharp teeth. Its paws then pushed down on the cold ground, ready to leap.

"Any ideas?" Fred asked, backing into the cave they had just come from.

Annie looked around and tightly pinched her nose, noticing that the three dark shadows had reorganised themselves.

"You can't escape," one of the shadows hissed, floating in and out of the darkness above.

The rats followed the children into the small cave, backing them into the corner. Annie's body was trembling all over. If the rats didn't eat them, the three shadowy figures would take their thoughts.

Although their options were limited, Annie remained focused as she scanned the cave until her eyes fell on something.

Whilst the shadows circled, ready to fly up the twosome's noses, she grabbed Fred's hand and jumped into the stream running through the cave.

Chapter twenty

Annie gasped; the water was deep and ice cold. It felt as though a million needles were pricking into her skin whilst standing inside a freezer.

Before she could catch her breath, the current instantly dragged the pair through the small hole in the wall that led into the tunnel. The water caused her light to go out, casting them into complete darkness.

"Fred!" she called out, her voice echoing off the walls, "grab hold of me; this ride's about to get wild!"

Fred grabbed hold. "Annie, do you ever think before you do something stupid?" he cried.

"No!" she yelled back. "It always seems like a great idea at the time!"

The current of the stream dragged them down a tunnel that bore deep into the rocks, seemingly disappearing into a never ending void.

Like a water slide, the stream suddenly fell downwards.

Annie and Fred's stomachs both did a somersault as they dropped with the stream, out of control, like a pair of anvils.

"Arhhh!" they cried, slipping down the stream, falling into a dark abyss.

Suddenly they dropped off the edge of an underground waterfall and into a pool of water at the bottom with a big *splash!*

Annie gasped again, her head breaking the surface. The water was like ice.

"Where are we?" Annie yelled through the dark.

"I don't know!" Fred cried back.

The current then wrapped its fingers around their bodies and dragged them off on another wild ride.

The stream pulled them down through the darkness, up and down, sideways and upside down. The children whizzed through the dangerous journey, not sure whether they would survive it.

But although the pair acquired bumps and bruises, they didn't receive cuts or broken bones. The water over thousands of years had ground down the surfaces of the rock so that they were polished and smooth.

The stream zigzagged, pulling the twosome with it. Annie's stomach jolted again and she didn't know how much more of the ferocious ride she could take, until suddenly a dazzling light appeared at the end.

The pair shot through a hole, fell with the waterfall on the other side, and with a *splash,* crashed into a pond.

The horrible sensation of instantly being surrounded by bubbles and water shooting up her nose made Annie instinctively flap aimlessly with her arms and kick wildly with her legs.

The moment her head broke the surface, she coughed and spluttered for several moments, before rubbing the water from her eyes. Finally Annie looked up, but what she saw came as a shock. Staring back at her were several puzzled faces.

Squinting through the glare of the late afternoon sun, her eyes having come accustomed to the pitch black of the tunnel, she looked around and noticed that the stream had emerged through a hole in the rock face above the small pond. She guessed they were in the middle of a public park, miles from the caves.

"Hi," she said with an innocent smile to the crowd. "Just thought I'd go for a quick swim."

She then turned to Fred, who was wet through. "You look like a drowned rat."

He wiped the water off his face. "Don't mention rats," he grunted, shuddering.

Chapter twenty-one

By the time the pair had made it back to the campsite it was nearing tea-time and Annie was puzzled. Having quickly visited the hospital on the way back, in order to check on Eira, the nurse had told the children that no one by that name had been brought in. But when Annie quizzed her, saying she had phoned for an ambulance, the nurse explained that when the paramedics had got to the house, they found it empty.

As Fred wondered off to let his parents know he was safe, Annie put the concern to the back of her mind, conscious she wasn't going to solve the disappearance of Eira Flynn there and then. Instead she dashed off to find her aunt.

But the moment her aunt spied her, the forty-year-old woman's face turned to a vision of shock. "What happened to you!" Aunt Grace gasped, noticing Annie's sodden and muddy clothes.

"Aunt Grace, you'll never guess what I did today and where I've been!" she cried. "It was amazing; I've just been deep inside a cave before being dragged through an underground stream!"

"A cave and an underground stream?" Aunt Grace shrieked.

"Yeah, and me and Fred fought with giant rats, huge bats and horrible Thought People. One of them is called The Thought Stealer and he's planning to feed on everyone's thoughts tonight, so he won't ever fade away into nothingness. He's –"

Aunt Grace cut her off. "Annie, what have I told you about telling tall stories?"

"But they're not," she insisted. "It really happened."

Aunt Grace lifted an eyebrow. "Annie, tell the truth. Where have you been all day?"

Annie let out a groan; she knew her aunt didn't believe her. In fact, she knew that no adult would believe her. This was the problem with all adults: they have lost their imaginations and only believe in reality. Even though Annie didn't believe in ghosts, because of what she had seen that morning she still had enough imagination left to believe in Thought People.

"Now come on," Aunt Grace urged, "where have you been all day?"

Finally Annie muttered, "Nowhere, I've been playing with Fred all afternoon."

"That's better," Aunt Grace smiled, tidying her niece's hair. "Now get changed into a clean T-shirt and shorts, then we can go have some tea. Oh and remember we're going to the fair tonight before watching the firework display that marks the end of the town's regatta; it's meant to be really good."

The fireworks, she thought. "I completely forgot."

"It's going to be great!" Aunt Grace exclaimed. "Everyone in the town's going to be there. We can have hot dogs and candyfloss, what do you think?"

Annie smiled. "That'll be great."

No sooner had Annie and Aunt Grace arrived at the dining hall than they were joined by Fred. He sat across the table and, with a mischievous smile, said, "So what do we do now?"

Annie looked to her aunt, who had a disapproving expression on her face, before turning to Fred and replying, "Nothing."

"What do you mean nothing?" Fred gasped. "We need to stop The Thought Stealer."

"What she means is that there'll be no more nonsense from the pair of you," Aunt Grace cut in. "We're going to the fair before watching the fireworks. If you want, you can come with us."

"Oh, I see," Fred muttered.

"That's better," Aunt Grace said. "Now I'm going to get some food."

She rose from her seat and started to walk to the serving area, before stopping. "Annie, are you not coming?"

"I'll just chat to Fred first," she replied. "You just go on ahead."

"Okay," Aunt Grace smiled before walking off.

The moment she was gone Annie leaned in and whispered, "We certainly are going after The Thought Stealer."

"But you said you were going to do nothing," Fred whispered back.

"Only because my aunt doesn't believe us," she explained. "She told me to forget about it. If she knew that I wanted to continue looking for this horrible Thought Person and his goons, she'd definitely try and stop me and that would mean no candyfloss or hot dogs tonight."

"Okay, so what do you reckon we should do?" Fred asked, rubbing his forehead. "If you haven't already forgotten we don't know where he is, how he plans to steal everyone's thoughts and how we'll be able to stop him."

"You're right and that's why we need to think sensibly about this," she said. "What do we know about him?"

"Err, I don't know," Fred replied.

"You're a great help," she scoffed.

"Then what do we know?" Fred countered.

"Okay," she said, putting her hands up. "We know he's made solely of horrible thoughts, we know that he steals all of a person's thoughts, leaving them like a zombie, and we know that he'll then consume the nasty thoughts before discarding the rest."

"So how will that help us stop him?" Fred asked.

There was a brief silence as Annie pondered the question. Finally she replied, "I'm not sure."

"What about science?" he suggested. "I thought you said it had all of the answers?"

"It does," Annie declared.

"Doesn't look like it from here," he argued.

"It does have the answers!" she shot back in a loud whisper. "As I keep telling you, we're just not looking in the right place!"

"Then where is the right place?" he asked.

"It's probably the simplest place," she thought out loud. "Now what else do we know about him?"

"Err… he's really cold," Fred suggested. "Maybe that'll help."

"That's it!" she shrieked, feeling a surge of energy fill her body.

"That's what?" Aunt Grace cut in.

Annie's face suddenly dropped. "Err… nothing."

"Oh, okay," Aunt Grace said, sitting down. "So what were you kids talking about?"

"Nothing," Annie replied, rising to her feet. "I'm just going to get some food now."

"Great!" Aunt Grace exclaimed. "Try the salad – it's really good."

"Will do," she replied, grabbing Fred by the back of his T-shirt and pulling him to his feet.

As Annie dragged Fred through the crowded dining hall towards the canteen, she whispered, "That's it."

"What is?" he asked.

"The fact that he's really cold," she explained. "That's exactly how we'll find him. If his hideout's in Brixham, we'll be able to pinpoint his exact location using science."

"How?" Fred asked.

"If we can find somewhere that monitors the temperatures around Brixham, the place that shows up to be really cold is probably where we'll find his secret hideout."

Fred nodded in appreciation. "That's very good and there was me thinking we could try and use magic."

"Now all we need to do is find somewhere that monitors temperatures," she said.

Chapter twenty-two

Having spoken to the receptionist at the campsite, Annie and Fred were pointed in the direction of the HM coastguard station situated near the inner harbour. They were told that if anywhere had the required technology, that place would have it since they monitored the coastline, responded to distress calls – by sending out the lifeboat and coastguard helicopter – and provided regular weather forecasts for sailors.

Knowing that her aunt was going for an early evening swim, Annie said that in the meantime she would enjoy the evening sunshine with Fred. Her aunt told her to stay out of trouble and not to be gone too long, otherwise she'd miss the fair and fireworks.

Limited on time, the pair swiftly retrieved their bikes from Grey Pebble Cove and rode to the HM coastguard station. She hoped she would be back before her aunt was out of the water.

"Annie, I don't know about this," Fred said.

"It'll be fine," she replied, locking up their bikes and walking up to the reception door. Fred followed her in and the pair were met by a man with short grey hair. He was wearing a smart uniform consisting of a white shirt, black trousers and shiny black shoes.

"Hello, children," the man said. He had a kind smile. "I'm Tom, one of the watch officers. What can I do for you?"

"Hi, my name's Annabelle Short and this is my friend Fredrick Greene," Annie explained, again using full names to seem all proper. "We're doing a summer project for school on the effects of global warming on the coastline of Devon. We've looked at the sea life, taken water samples and even looked at the local history books to see what the coastline was like a hundred years ago. But what we haven't managed to get is the different temperatures in and around Brixham, and that was why we were wondering whether you could help?"

"And how can I help with that?" Tom asked.

"Well, because you send out regular weather forecasts I suspect you have equipment that allows you to monitor temperatures," Annie said. "I was wondering whether we could look at it."

A smile appeared across Tom's face. "Sure," he said, "if it's going towards helping your school project how can I say no."

"Great!" Annie exclaimed, turning to Fred and winking.

The boy responded with a disapproving shake of the head.

Tom led the twosome into the control room, which was full of an array of computer terminals and communication and monitoring equipment, all manned by people wearing similar uniforms.

"This is where we monitor the coastline and reply to distress calls," Tom explained.

"Very interesting," Annie replied, rubbing her chin, trying to look genuinely interested.

Tom led the two children to a computer terminal, which had on the screen a satellite image of the coastline. He sat down in front of the keyboard, selected the weather program and started to type.

In an instant, several charts and numbers appeared on the screen. "Okay, kids, what would you like to know?"

Annie stepped up. "Can you monitor the different temperatures in and around Brixham?"

"Sure," he replied, punching a series of commands into the keyboard which brought up a map of the town. "This is a satellite image of Brixham. By selecting the program that monitors temperatures we can detect which areas are hot and which are cold."

"By different colours," Annie cut in, having read about it in a science book.

"Exactly!" Tom exclaimed. "Hot temperatures show up as red and cold as blue. The darker the shade of blue, the colder it is."

The watch officer tapped several more commands into the keyboard and, sure enough, the majority of Brixham's landmass glowed red, whilst the water appeared as blue.

Annie looked at the screen. "This is brilliant."

"As you can see, even though it's the early evening, because it's summer the town's still hot, having not fully cooled down from the onslaught of the summer sun throughout the day," Tom explained.

Hearing this Annie smiled to herself; this technology was exactly what she needed to locate The Thought Stealer.

Not wishing to waste any more time her eyes scanned the screen for traces of dark blue. She quickly noticed that the water temperature became cooler the further out to sea it was and at the end of the breakwater there was a deep red dot – which she assumed was the lighthouse. There were also traces of orange on the headland overlooking the harbour, which she assumed was the heat coming off the machinery that was running the fair.

She continued to search and it didn't take long to find what she was looking for. She pointed to a small dark blue dot that appeared on the screen. "Can you zoom in on that?" she asked.

"Sure," Tom replied, typing in several more commands.

The image homed in on the dark blue dot.

"That's strange," Tom grunted.

"What is?" Annie asked.

"That blue dot is saying that the temperature is very cold," he explained.

"So what's wrong with that?" Fred asked. "Maybe it's someone's fridge."

"Unlikely," Tom said. "The cold spot's situated just outside the mouth of the harbour."

"The mouth of the harbour?" Annie questioned.

"Yeah," Tom said, walking up to the massive windows that looked out over the harbour and out into Torbay. Annie and Fred joined him.

Tom then pointed to the mouth of the harbour. "That's where your cold spot is," he said, "where that tall ship's anchored."

Although the bright red evening sun was making her squint, Annie looked. But the moment she saw the small ship, which was tugging at its anchor in the light swell, she recognised it immediately. It was the tall ship that had been anchored off Grey Pebble Cove earlier.

She turned to Tom. "What's a tall ship doing in the harbour?"

Tom answered, "They come in all the time, since they're used quite a lot to train young people how to sail."

"Are you sure that's where the cold spot is?" Annie asked.

The man walked back to the computer monitor and examined the satellite image a second time. "Yep, but I'm sure it's a mistake with the equipment. It'll need mending."

"Why do you say that?" Fred probed, knowing quite a bit about fixing computers.

"Simple, the ship's appearing as a dark blue blob on the screen, whereas the water surrounding it is light blue," the watch officer detailed.

"So what does that mean?" Fred asked.

Before Tom could explain further, Annie cut in. "If you went to junior science club you'd know."

"Well, Professor Einstein, can you explain?" Fred pouted.

"What it's saying is that the ship's colder than the sea surrounding it, because the colder it is, the darker the colour will appear on the screen," she said. "Simple."

"Great, Einstein," Fred mocked again, "but why would that mean there's a fault with the machine?"

Tom was about to answer when Annie cut in a second time. "Because the ship should be quite hot, since it has absorbed the sun's rays that have been beating down on it for the entire day. However, the heat of the sun beating down on the water's surface wouldn't have the same effect."

"Surely the sun would heat the sea and make it hot as well," Fred argued.

Annie raised an eyebrow. "If that's true, then why's it always cold when you jump in the sea?"

The boy shrugged his shoulders.

"Because there's so much water in the bay, the sun can't heat it all. It's like trying to boil a cup of cold water by putting it under a light bulb. It's never going to happen. And that's why the instruments appear to be wrong. The ship shouldn't appear to be colder than the water that surrounds it," she detailed.

A broad grin widened across Tom's face. "That's very good!" he bellowed, clapping his hands. "If only all kids took the same amount of interest in science as you do, instead of sitting in front of the TV scoffing junk food."

Annie blushed. "It's something I love. Science holds all of the answers."

"That's great," Tom exclaimed, his grin remaining. He then printed out a sheet that had temperature data on it and passed it to the children. "Is there anything else I can help the both of you with?"

Annie looked to Fred and then back to the watch officer. "No, that's fine. I think we've seen all that we needed to see."

Chapter twenty-three

While the two children sat on the wall that ran around the inner harbour, Annie continued to stare at the old tall ship. She was fascinated by it; a small ship with three massive masts, a bow sprit pointing out in front like a spear and a flag dancing in the light breeze at the stern.

It seemed wholly out of place; a hundred-year-old vessel that was sharing the sea with diesel guzzling trawlers, fast power boats and expensive designer yachts. The only ship that looked marginally similar was the replica of the *Golden Hind,* which was a tourist attraction berthed in the corner of the inner harbour. She had been for a tour on it with her aunt a few days earlier.

"What's the plan?" Fred asked.

Annie finally looked round, a mischievous grin painted across her face.

"I don't like the look of that smile," he muttered. "Can't we just go home?"

Annie shook her head.

"Annie, we've got into enough trouble today already!" Fred said.

"We're going to check it out," Annie explained. "I bet that's where The Thought Stealer has his secret hideout – it's perfect. No one would ever suspect a tall ship of wrong doing."

"Maybe it's just a normal tall ship," Fred suggested. "It could just be like Tom said – being used to give children sailing experience."

"Whether or not that's the case, I'm going to find out," Annie declared.

Fred rubbed his face. "Annie, I only met you this morning and in that time I've almost had my mind sucked dry twice, been in a battle with a medieval knight before being chased by giant rats and bats. Going with you is pure madness." He looked at his watch. "Besides, it's almost seven o'clock – we really should be getting back."

Annie looked deep into the young boy's eyes. "Fred, we know that this Thought Stealer character is planning something awful and if we want to find out what it is, we need to look on that ship," she whispered. "And the fact that the sun's starting to go down means we'll have to act fast."

"Annie, it's too dangerous," he argued, the lines visible above his brow.

"So you're not coming?" she asked.

"No," he replied, "and neither are you."

"But, Fred," Annie insisted.

Before she could muster another word, the voice returned. *Annabelle, you mustn't give up.*

Like had happened before, it seemed to have come from everywhere. The cold chill returned. *Who said that?* she wondered, looking at the many people lazily strolling by. She then turned to Fred. "Did you hear that?"

"Hear what?" the boy asked.

"Never mind," she muttered before looking at the families kneeling over the harbour wall holding crabbing lines. *Was it one of them?* she thought.

However, they were more intent on pulling crabs from the rocks beneath the surface and storing them in brightly coloured buckets.

She then looked at the people sitting on the benches. But they were either chatting to one another, or soaking up the last of the sun.

Who could have said that? her mind asked again.

However, the answer never came and she was pulled from her thoughts by Fred. "Annie, I'm not going out to that ship and neither are you," he ordered. "Anyway, how're you going to get out there? It's a long swim."

There was a glint in the corner of the young girl's eye. "I've got an idea."

Not giving Fred the chance to argue, she jumped onto her bike and rode off in the direction of the breakwater and lifeboat station.

Fred jumped onto his bike and gave chase. "Annie!" he shouted. "Let's go back to the campsite. We can think of a plan back there!"

Annie continued to ride. "No, we have to go out and have a look around the ship!" she shouted back. "I'm sure it was the one we saw earlier off the cove and I'm sure it's being used to transport that massive yellow crystal!"

Fred rode up next to her and, trying not to hit the many people walking by, said. "How are you going to get out there anyway?"

"That's easy," she replied, continuing to cycle up the harbour walkway. People yelled at her to be more careful.

The pair finally came to a small building in the corner of the harbour.

Fred pulled up and read the sign on the side of the building. "Canoeing?" he asked.

Annie nodded. "Aunt Grace and I have had a few lessons this week; they're really good," she said, locking up her bike before walking inside.

After a quick chat with the instructor – who recognised her immediately – Annie dashed outside and told Fred it was okay for them to join the next lesson.

Chapter twenty-four

Half an hour later and Annie was wearing a lifejacket over her T-shirt and a bright yellow helmet, and her shorts were wet from the water in the bottom of the canoe. But she didn't mind though, since she was bobbing around in the harbour with the instructor and eight teenagers.

She had tried to persuade Fred to join her, but being a big baby he'd refused and chosen to wait by the harbour.

"Okay, everyone, we're going to paddle out to the mouth of the harbour and play some games! So follow me!" the instructor, who was a young woman with sandy blonde hair and grey eyes called Ellen, ordered. She was fresh out of college, making her no older than eighteen.

Annie waited for Ellen and the eight canoes to get underway first. She wanted to bring up the rear so no one would see what she was up to. Furthermore, because the teenagers seemed to be quite experienced, she didn't want them to notice that she was a beginner and thus keep an eye on her.

While she paddled out with the group to the mouth of the harbour, her eyes were drawn to the tall ship and she almost bumped into a yacht that was moored to a buoy.

"Wow!" she shrieked, negotiating the little canoe back on course.

One of the teenagers looked round. "You okay?" he asked.

Annie smiled. "Yeah, fine."

The teenager smiled back before continuing to paddle towards their destination.

In no time at all, the group was floating in the harbour's mouth, only yards from the tall ship.

Being so close to the vessel, Annie's hunch that this was The Thought Stealer's hideout was heightened, owing to the cold chill that occupied the air around its hull and the fact that it seemed to be devoid of a soul. It was like a ghost ship.

The cogs in her mind started to turn. If she was to get to the ship unnoticed, she'd need a distraction so that Ellen's attention would be focused on something other than her.

"Okay!" Ellen yelled. "I want you to line up your canoes and hold onto each other! Then what I want you to do is, one by one, stand up and run along the line of canoes! The person who makes it from one end to the other without falling in wins!" she announced, waving to the safety boat bobbing on the surface near by. The person on the boat waved back, letting her know this was going to be done safely.

Everyone manoeuvred their canoes so that they were lined up next to each other. Annie made sure she was on the end.

"Okay, Annie!" Ellen shouted. "You're first! Run from one end to the other!"

"Err, I can't, I've hurt my foot!" she lied, not wishing to be parted from her canoe. A plan was forming in her mind.

"Alright, Bobby, you go!" she yelled to the teenager in the canoe next to Annie's. He was short and chubby.

The young boy unsteadily stood up and tried to run across the line of canoes. But he managed to get to the canoe opposite before losing his footing, slipping and falling into the water with a *splash!*

Everyone laughed, except for Annie. She was more interested in pulling the plug out of the bottom of the empty canoe.

Bobby swam round to his canoe and climbed back inside. But the moment he did, he shrieked, "Ellen, my canoe's sinking!"

In the space of several seconds Bobby was bobbing up and down in the water and the small canoe was resting inside the safety boat, upside down with water draining out of it. All eyes were on it and no one saw Annie paddle off towards the tall ship.

She went as fast as she could, her arms burning like fire, and she didn't stop until she was pulling up next to the ship.

The white hull loomed above like a massive wooden wall and Annie paddled round to the rope ladder dangling over the stern, dipping in the water. Being as quiet as she could, she tied up the canoe, removed her helmet and climbed onto the stern deck. But what she saw took her breath away. It was ghastly!

On the deck was a crewmember and she was standing still, eyes wide open, in a trance-like state.

Chapter twenty-five

"This is horrible," she breathed, the words barely leaving her lips as her eyes moved from the crewmember in front to the other crewmembers standing nearby. She couldn't draw her eyes away from them. The crew, who were made up of young adults, were frozen. Fear was imprinted on their faces, since the colour had been drained from their cheeks and their mouths were wide open.

Suddenly Annie became aware that The Thought Stealer must have been on board. He had to be, nothing else could have done this to the crew. He'd fed on their thoughts and now he had enough energy to do what he pleased.

Annie pinched her nose, quickly dashed across the deck, darted into the wheelhouse and dived under the chart table. She looked around, hoping she hadn't been seen. But there wasn't a soul nearby, so after a short while she decided to investigate further.

Tiptoeing down the wooden steps and into the galley, her mind insisted, *This is a real stupid idea, you should turn back! You've already been captured by The Thought Stealer today. You mightn't be lucky enough to escape a second time.*

However, her curiosity got the better of her and she continued deeper into the bowels of the ship.

124

But the moment she arrived at the galley, her breath was again taken away. There were a few more crewmembers, all frozen like statues. Some were standing holding plates, whilst others were sitting behind tables with knives and forks in their hands. One was even sitting motionless with a fork in his mouth. Again, the look of fear on their faces was palpable.

Aware she couldn't help them, Annie continued deeper into the belly of the ship, walking down the passageway to the decks below – the air turning colder with every step. She shivered and the goosebumps returned.

She got to the door at the end and when she pushed it open she instantly knew that this was the place she was searching for.

There was a large storage room and resting on the deck was the same large yellow crystal she'd observed earlier that day in the caves.

Her heart pounding, she slowly walked towards the crystal and examined it. On closer inspection, it was dark yellow in colour. The light somehow filtering through the cracks in the wooden hatch in the ceiling caused it to glisten. Because the room was on the lowest deck of the ship, she presumed that on the other side of the hatch was a shaft that led to the top deck.

She continued to gaze at the crystal and wondered what it would be used for. But before she could think any more the room turned cold, like a winter's day. She looked up, and appearing from the darkness in the reaches of the room was a shadow.

Its jagged edges and the cold chill surrounding it left Annie in no doubt it was The Thought Stealer.

She quickly hid behind several wooden boxes in the corner and held her breath, hoping the horrible creature wouldn't hear. She then watched, transfixed, as the three cloaked figures also emerged from the shadows.

"Now it's time to test the crystal and make sure that it's ready to be used tonight on the humans," The Thought Stealer rasped, his voice sounding like an out of tune banjo. "All we need is someone to test it on."

Who's he going to test it on? Annie wondered, holding her nose and looking around. *Are there more members of the crew yet to have their minds sucked dry?*

The Thought Stealer looked round before stopping and pointing his twig-like finger directly at the door at the other end of the room. "Bring out the final prisoner," he ordered to one of the cloaked figures.

The cloaked figured disappeared through the door and returned with a teenage boy. Annie instantly presumed that the boy with short ginger hair, pale skin and a pot belly was the last remaining teenage crew member.

Chapter twenty-six

Unable to move her eyes away from the scene unfolding, Annie just watched as The Thought Stealer's fingers snaked along the deck and wrapped around the boy's ankles.

"Get off me!" the boy shrieked, trying without luck to prise The Thought Stealer's fingers off his ankles; they were wrapped too tightly.

Suddenly he dragged the boy along the deck towards the yellow crystal.

"No!" the boy howled, digging his short nails into the deck.

This is horrid! Annie thought, beads of sweat trickling down from her brow. The anticipation of what she was about to witness stopped her body from moving.

The Thought Stealer then moved closer to the boy, who was now sitting completely still, paralysed by fear. "The crystal in front of you has come from deep within the rocks around this part of the coast. But it isn't like a normal crystal; it's very special indeed. It's called a Thinking Crystal," The Thought Stealer hissed. "You see, when a Thinking Crystal is exposed to light, it will attract thoughts. When someone forgets something, unless a Thought Person gets that thought, the redundant thought will be attracted to these crystals and trapped inside. Black coloured crystals attract good thoughts, white ones attract bad thoughts and yellow ones attract every type of thought. I would have preferred to find a white crystal, but the yellow ones were the only ones that I was able to find."

The monster continued, "But the small ones are no use to me, since they only attract thoughts that have escaped from humans heads. But the big ones, like the one here, are very different. You see the bigger the crystal, the more powerful it is. The big crystal that is in front of you doesn't just attract thoughts that have escaped from human's heads. When exposed to light, it will suck the thoughts right out of the head of a person who is standing near to it, leaving their mind completely empty. The thoughts will be sucked out through their noses. When I touch the crystal, which is full of the stolen thoughts, the bad thoughts will be transferred to me, adding to my power."

The boy's eyes widened, worried about what that meant for him.

The Thought Stealer continued. "Being buried deep within the rocks, only lit by the dim candlelight, this crystal was quite harmless, but if it were exposed to intense light then it would become a million times more powerful."

Her heart pounding, Annie almost gasped but put her hand over her mouth. *If he eats all of the bad thoughts that the crystal steals, then he'll have enough bad thoughts to attain critical mass. If that happens he'll never fade away into nothingness and*

128

instead he'll become an unstoppable monster, she thought.

Realising what was in front of her, Annie kicked herself. Without giving it much thought, she'd steamed into another deadly situation. This led her to wonder how she and the teenager were going to get off the ship alive.

Her mind quickly moved to Fred; it was a good job he hadn't come, otherwise he would have suffered the same fate that was about to befall her when The Thought Stealer no doubt discovered her.

Annie turned back to the scene in front and watched as The Thought Stealer hovered for several moments, before wrapping his hands around the crystal.

One of the cloaked figures prepared to open the hatch in the ceiling, allowing the light outside to excite the crystal and cause it to start attracting thoughts like a big magnet.

"You see, little boy," The Thought Stealer hissed, "you'll become the first person who'll have all of his thoughts taken in this way. In a matter of moments your mind will be empty – sucked dry. I'll then be able to feed on the bad thoughts caught by the crystal and discard the rest."

This can't be happening! Annie's mind screamed, thinking of all of the lives that The Thought Stealer was going to end that evening. *I can't believe I won't be able to stop him.*

If that didn't make her feel bad, the realisation of where he was planning to use the dreadful crystal did. It was obvious and had been staring her in the face all day long. There was only one place where enough people were going to be congregating: the fair and the firework display. It would be taking place later that evening on the top of the headland overlooking the harbour.

Unable to move, she watched as one of the cloaked figures readied to open the hatch and expose the crystal to the light from the evening sun, which was just setting over the hills.

Chapter twenty-seven

But the moment the hatch was opened and the sun's rays filtered down the shaft into the room, something odd happened. The crystal didn't come to life.

Instead one of the ship's large white sails fell from the mast hanging over the hatch and in an instant completely covered the crystal, The Thought Stealer, his goons and the teenager, trapping them underneath.

Annie was stunned, unable to work out what had just happened, until she dashed from behind the boxes and ran over to the crumpled sail. She then looked up through the open hatch to the mast high above. Hanging from the rigging of the mast was Fred.

Shocked, she yelled, "What are you doing up there?"

Fred smiled. "Thought you might have needed my help so I borrowed a small dinghy from the inner harbour and paddled out here!" he explained. "Good job I did, because having dashed down the passageway I noticed that there was a bit of trouble."

Annie was relieved. She quickly looked at the crumpled sail and, seeing the horrid Thought People moving around beneath, decided it was the best time to get off the vessel.

She pulled back the part of the sail covering the now confused boy and dragged him to his feet.

She looked up at Fred. "Meet me on the deck!" she explained, before charging off down the small passageway with the teenager in tow.

In no time at all Annie and the teenager were standing on the deck with Fred.

Suddenly the teenager spoke. "What's going on?"

"There's no time to explain," Annie replied. "All you need to know is that my name's Annie and this is Fred and there is a very angry creature called The Thought Stealer below deck with his horrible goons."

The relief on the boy's face was evident. It was nice to see a couple of friendly faces. "Okay," the boy replied. "Oh, by the way, my name's Adam."

Fred smiled at the boy, before turning to Annie. "So what's the plan?"

Annie peered at the dinghy tied to the stern. "We get as far away from here as we can!"

"I'm not going to argue with that," Fred replied.

The threesome darted for the stern to make their escape. But before they could get there, a ghastly shadow with jagged edges blocked their path!

Annie, Fred and the teenager stood motionless for several moments, watching a mouth form in the middle of the shadow. "Did you think that sail could stop me?" The Thought Stealer growled, swooping down and picking the dinghy out of the

132

water with ease. He carried it through the air and tossed it down the shaft. With a thunderous crash the dinghy hit the deck in the storage room.

Seeing their means of escape taken away, the threesome turned and charged off down the deck towards the bow of the ship.

The Thought Stealer gave chase.

He flew down on Annie and swept her off her feet, causing her to tumbled onto her knees. Despite the pain shooting through her body, she jumped up and continued to race for the bow of the vessel. Fred and Adam were still on their feet.

"I think we should jump into the water and hope that monster can't swim!" Annie panted.

"That's not one of your better ideas!" Fred replied.

"Got any better ones?" Annie fired back.

"No!" he replied.

"Then let's jump for it!" she yelled.

Annie, Fred and Adam jumped over the side of the ship.

But they didn't fall into the water with a splash.

Instead, they found themselves hanging upside down in mid-air. The Thought Stealer was holding them by their ankles.

Chapter twenty-eight

In no time at all The Thought Stealer's goons had removed the crystal from the ship and locked Annie, Fred and Adam inside the main storage room.

"This isn't good," Annie muttered, dashing over to the door and trying to open it. It was locked.

Adam did the same with the door at the opposite end, before looking round. "Locked!" he shouted.

Annie then suddenly blurted out, "Fred, I'm really sorry!"

"For what?" Fred asked.

"For putting you in so much danger," she explained. "I was so selfish in asking you to come with me on this adventure – I didn't think about your safety. I've steamed into two situations now without thinking, which have resulted in us getting captured."

Fred smiled. "It's okay."

Annie couldn't understand it. "Give me one good reason why it's okay?"

"Because I've really enjoyed spending the day with you!" the boy explained. "I think you're great."

Although this wasn't the best time to have the conversation, Annie asked, "But you could have had a better day with your friends."

"Annie, no I couldn't," he said.

"Why not?" the girl asked.

"Because I don't have any friends!" Fred snapped.

In spite of the danger, Fred continued. "Every day of this summer's been rubbish. My mum won't let me go to the beach on my own, because it's too dangerous, I've had no one to play around with and all this happened because I stood up for what was right. But when you turned up it was brilliant. I found someone who wanted to spend the day with me."

Annie was stunned. "Fred, I don't understand," she whispered. "Why would you have no friends? You're really nice."

But before the conversation could continue, Adam cut in. "Now isn't the best time to discuss this!"

Annie realised the teenager was right. They had to get off the ship, so she started to think. *Why's The Thought Stealer left us locked inside the ship instead of killing us?* she wondered. *Surely he knows the moment we escape we'll try and stop him.*

This question puzzled her as she looked round at the contents of the room. Her eyes finally fixed on Fred's dinghy, which The Thought Stealer had discarded there. She wandered over to the tatty little wooden boat and read the nameplate on the hull. It was called *Pisces*.

"So why's The Thought Stealer just left us here?" Fred asked, joining her.

She replied. "I don't –"

However, before she could finish her sentence the ship suddenly jolted and the three youngsters were thrown to the deck.

"What was that?" Fred gasped, pulling himself to his feet.

"I'm not sure," Annie replied, right before the ship jolted again, this time more violently.

All of a sudden the ship began to rock from side to side and Annie, Fred and Adam were thrown across the deck, where they all crashed into the wall, right before they slid across the deck to the other side.

"This is horrible!" Fred yelled. "I feel like I'm inside a toy ship that's being rattled by an angry child!"

"I think it's The Thought Stealer!" Annie shrieked, trying to grab hold of something to stop herself sliding all over the place.

The rocking of the ship continued relentlessly for several more moments before it stopped, leaving the three children lying on the floor feeling well and truly sea sick.

As though they'd been inside a washing machine, she looked over at Fred. He was also lying on the floor, his face as pale as a bed sheet.

Annie then unsteadily rose to her feet and staggered over to Fred. But before she got to the young boy she was suddenly knocked off her feet, as a tremor rattled through the ship.

"What was that?" Fred gasped.

"It seems like something's rammed the underneath of the ship," Annie replied, right before another tremor shook the ship. It felt as though a battering ram was being smacked against the underside of the hull.

Annie, Fred and Adam froze as the ship trembled again. But this time the floor boards rattled.

Suddenly there was an almighty *bang!* as The Thought Stealer impacted with the underside of the ship with such force that the old wood gave way.

In an instant, water gushed in through the hole that had been made in the hull, splashing over the deck and around the children's feet like an unstoppable tide.

"This isn't good!" Adam yelled, the water level quickly rising above his ankles.

Fred looked around. "We're trapped!"

"I know!" Annie replied, watching as more and more water poured in through the hole in the deck.

The situation was awful. They were trapped inside a ship that was now quickly filling with liquid.

Annie waded through the water that was now at knee height. "Any suggestions?" she asked Fred.

"I thought you were the one with all of the answers!" he replied.

She then turned to Adam. "Do you have any suggestions?"

The teenager shook his head. "No."

Annie's heart was pounding. With the water level quickly rising she had to think fast. "The doors are locked and the only way out is through the hole in the floor! But unless we can breathe underwater, then that's not an option," she said.

"That's it!" Fred cried, looking at the dinghy now floating in the water, which was now waist high.

"That's what?" Annie asked.

"The hole in the floor!" he exclaimed.

Annie's heart dropped. "We can't get out that way," she pointed out. "Even if we could hold our breaths long enough to swim under the ship and to safety, The Thought Stealer would be waiting for us when we surface."

Fred smiled. "Annie, who's saying anything about having to hold our breaths?"

The girl was puzzled. "What do you mean?"

"What I mean is that I have an idea," Fred gasped, wading through the water, which had risen to neck level, towards the *Pisces.*

The small dinghy was now floating on the surface.

"Annie, Adam, give me a hand!" Fred ordered.

In the space of several seconds the water became too high to wade through, so she swam over to the dinghy. She grabbed hold of the side, trying to get in.

Fred took her arm. "Annie, we're not going to get inside!" he explained. "We're going to tip it upside down."

"What!" she gasped. "That's stupid!"

"Trust me!" Fred yelled, the water almost lapping against the ceiling.

There was very little air left in the room and Annie had to make a snap decision. Although what Fred had suggested was absolutely stupid, it was the only suggestion available. "Okay, hotshot!" she shouted, treading water. "Let's go for it!"

The threesome grabbed hold of the side of the dinghy and together tipped it completely over, so that it was floating on the surface upside down.

"Now what?" she asked, the water lapping against the ceiling.

Fred didn't answer. All he did was grab Annie's arm and pull her below the surface.

Although the girl was shocked, she didn't fight him. It was a strange sensation, but she completely trusted the young boy.

Fred pulled Annie under the upturned dinghy and to her surprise the inside was filled with air.

Annie took a deep breath and through the dark she could just about make out Fred's grinning face. Adam quickly joined them.

"The inside of the *Pisces* has trapped a pocket of air for us to breathe," he explained, the keel of the upturned dinghy now bumping against the ceiling.

"We haven't got long before the air turns foul, so we need to work fast."

"This is great, but what about the other members of the crew? Although they've had their minds sucked dry they'll still drown when this ship sinks," Annie pointed out.

"No they won't," Adam replied.

"Why not?" Annie wondered.

"Because the harbour isn't very deep," the teenager explained. "The ship will hit the harbour's bed before the decks containing the rest of the crew are flooded. Since this deck's at the bottom, it's the only deck that'll be flooded."

With the weight of the safety of the crew off her mind, she turned to Fred. "So what's the plan?"

"Trust me," he said, before disappearing under the surface.

Annie waited nervously for Fred to return. And when he did he was carrying a small anchor. Using all the strength he could muster, he lifted the weight above his head and propped it under the seat of the dinghy.

Annie suddenly realised what Fred had done. "That's a great plan!" she exclaimed with a smile.

The weight of the anchor caused the *Pisces* to sink down through the hole in the deck, where it sank below the ship until the threesome felt the muddy bed of Brixham harbour beneath their feet.

"Okay, what now?" Annie asked.

"Considering we have a sinking ship in the water above our heads, I suggest we move," Fred said.

Holding the dinghy above their heads, Annie, Fred and Adam walked along the bed of the harbour until they were sure that they were away from the ship and The Thought Stealer's prying eyes. Fred then let the anchor drop into the mud below and allowed the dinghy and themselves to float to the surface.

The moment the dinghy broke the surface, Annie looked over and watched the lower level of the tall ship disappear beneath the water.

Adam then turned to the children. "Whoever the pair of you are, thanks for saving my life."

"Well, if it wasn't for Fred you would've been done for," Annie replied.

Adam looked at the young boy. "Thanks."

Annie then turned to Fred. "You okay?"

He nodded and spoke. "That was a bit of a close one."

Chapter twenty-nine

It had gone eight o'clock and Annie and Fred were sitting inside the lifeboat station wrapped in warm blankets. The pair were wet through and had been shivering since the crew of the lifeboat had fished them out of the water. Adam, however, wasn't with the two children since he'd stayed on the lifeboat as his zombified friends were rescued from the tall ship.

A crewman, who was dressed in an orange dry suit and lifejacket, passed the two children a cup of hot chocolate each.

"Thanks," they both muttered, wrapping their cold fingers around the hot plastic cups.

The man smiled before wandering off to fetch a stack of paperwork.

"So why don't you have any friends?" Annie asked. "I can't understand it – you're so nice."

Fred gazed into his drink. "You remember when my mum said this morning that I did the right thing?"

Annie nodded.

"Well, she was referring to what happened on the first day of the summer holidays," the boy explained. "You see my friends fell out with me and they haven't spoken to me since."

"Oh," Annie whispered. "So what happened?"

"We went to play tennis at the leisure centre, but when we finished my friends Mark and Pete decided they wanted to keep the tennis rackets they'd borrowed," Fred explained. "I thought it was dishonest and tried to make them take them back."

Annie scratched her chin and then asked, "Did they take the rackets back?"

"No," Fred explained. "They attacked me with them before calling me a Goody Two Shoes. We haven't spoken since."

Annie was about to speak, but Fred continued. "You know, if I had known that I would've spent most of my summer alone, I wouldn't have tried to make them take the rackets back," he explained.

"Fred, don't say that," Annie said, rubbing his arm. She noticed he was upset and who could blame him. He'd done the right thing and all it had served to do was bite him in the backside.

"But it's true," Fred insisted. "There's nothing worse than living by the seaside and having no one to enjoy it with."

"You have me to enjoy it with," Annie pointed out.

Fred wiped his eyes. "Yeah, but you're going back to Leicester soon, leaving me on my own again. I might as well say sorry to those boys and at least I'll have friends again."

Hearing this, Annie changed her tone. "Don't you dare!"

This caught Fred by surprise. "Huh?"

"You go back to them and you'll be losing the very things I like about you," she argued.

The boy was puzzled.

"Fred, what those boys seemed to hate about you is what I love," she explained. "Since this morning I've met someone who's honest, decent and kind, and although I'll be going home to Leicester, you'll be coming up to visit."

Hearing this Fred's face lit up. "Really?"

"Definitely," she said.

Fred was about to say how much he'd like that, when the lifeboat crewman returned and knelt down. "So, do you children care to tell me what happened out there?" he asked.

Annie took a sip of her drink, but because she was so cold the hot fluid bit sharply at her lips. Finally she spoke. "You won't believe us."

The crewman ran his fingers over the stubble on his chin. "Try me."

"Okay, well it all started this morning," she explained. But before Annie got any further, she stopped as she spied a familiar person walk through the door. It was her Aunt Grace, who was then followed by Fred's parents.

"Annie!" Aunt Grace shrieked, seeing her niece in such a state. She raced over and wrapped her arms around the young girl.

It felt like her aunt was going to squeeze the life out of her, but she didn't mind though. She loved her aunt and was pleased to see her since she was a little shaken up after almost being killed.

"What happened?" her aunt demanded.

144

Annie was about to fill her in on the details but stopped. She knew her aunt would never believe her, so she lied. "Fred and I went out on a canoeing lesson, but we got lost and almost ended up being drowned when that tall ship sank. It was horrible."

Her aunt pulled herself away and examined her niece for cuts and bruises. "But you're okay now?" she asked.

Annie nodded before looking over to Fred, who was being squeezed just as tightly by his parents. "I'm fine," she lied.

Annie didn't like lying, but here it was necessary. If she told the truth, her aunt wouldn't let her out of her sight and that would mean she wouldn't be able to stop The Thought Stealer. She needed to play it cool. "Aunt, I know what'll cheer me up."

"Whatever you want," her aunt replied, still checking her niece.

"Can we go to the fair and watch the fireworks?" Annie asked.

"Are you sure you're up to it?" her aunt said, checking her niece.

Annie nodded. "Oh, and can Fred come along as well?"

Chapter thirty

By the time Annie and Fred got to the fair, having been back to the campsite to change into clean clothes, which consisted of warm jumpers over T-shirts and shorts, it had gone nine o'clock. Now the stars twinkled clearly in the night-time sky and the place was jam-packed with people of all shapes and sizes. Annie could hardly see further than a few feet in front but for a thick sea of bodies.

"So what ride do you kids want to go on first?" Aunt Grace asked. "The waltzers or the dodgems?"

Annie looked up at her aunt. She didn't want to go on a ride; she was more interested in locating The Thought Stealer. "Can we get something to eat first please?"

"Sure," Aunt Grace replied.

As they weaved through the mass of people she turned to Fred. "This is worse than I thought. If The Thought Stealer uses the power of the crystal here, hundreds of people will have all of their thoughts sucked out of their heads. And with all these people around, finding where the crystal will be placed is going to be impossible."

"Annie, because it's dark surely the crystal will be useless," the boy pointed out.

Annie had thought about this and replied, "He must be intending to create a source of light from somewhere."

"Good point," Fred replied. He then jumped up and down, trying to peer over the sea of heads. "This is useless," he gasped. "Looking for where The Thought Stealer's positioned the crystal is like looking for a needle in a haystack."

"What are you doing, Fred?" Aunt Grace cut in.

"Err, just trying to see what rides there are," he explained.

"I see," Aunt Grace replied, before turning towards the hot dog stand and groaning. There was a massive queue. She turned back to the two children. "You kids go on a couple of the rides while I queue up," she said, passing Annie a handful of coins. "I'll come and find you both when I've been served."

The whiff of the hot dogs, burgers and fried onions made Annie's mouth water. Although it smelt delicious, her aunt being stuck in a queue would provide a great opportunity to search the fairground unhindered. She turned to Fred. "Come on, we'll have a go on the dodgems."

"That's a great idea," Fred replied, playing along.

Annie looked at her aunt. "I'll have extra tomato sauce on my hot dog and Fred'll have extra onions," she said.

Before Fred could say he didn't like onions, Annie dragged him off into the crowds.

As soon as the two children were out of sight of Aunt Grace, Annie turned to Fred. "I suggest we split up. I'll search the fairground and you can search the green where the fireworks are set to go off."

"That's a good plan," he replied. "But what should I do if I manage to find the crystal?"

"Try and think of something on the way. And look out for three figures dressed in red cloaks," she suggested before wandering off.

Annie fought her way through the masses of people. *Okay, Annie,* she thought, *you need to be systematic about this if you're going to stop The Thought Stealer.*

She scratched her head before looking through the crowds of people and spying one of the rides. The flashing lights, spinning carriages and whirring horn was enough to make anyone feel sick before they jumped onto the ride, especially with copious amounts of burgers, candyfloss and fizzy drinks sloshing around in the bottom of their stomach. But Annie loved the waltzers – her aunt was planning to take her on the ride.

Her eyes then moved to the helter-skelter and then to the big wheel. The attractions were sparkling with flashing lights and were full of people.

She then looked at the other rides. First the American eggs, then the ghost house and finally the dodgems. But she couldn't see any sign of the large yellow Thinking Crystal.

Oh no! her mind suddenly cried. *It must be under one of the rides. It has to be... nicely hidden from view, ready to be brought out when the time is right!*

Annie quickly raced past the people, trying to find someone who worked for the fairground. *There must be someone here who can stop the fair and get everyone away from the place!*

Annie's eyes shifted from one person to the next. She saw families eating candyfloss, teenagers queuing for the scariest rides and people attempting to win cuddly toys by trying to throw hoops over glass bottles. But there was no one who seemed like they could help.

She kept looking though, before finding four people dressed as clowns. One was pumping helium into colourful balloons from a metal cylinder, whilst the others were handing the balloons out.

She raced over to the people with curly bright green hair, white faces, large red noses, baggy clothes and big red boots. "Excuse me!" she yelled to the four clowns.

One of the clowns looked round. "Yes?" he chuckled.

Annie panted. "I know this is going to sound a bit silly, but being clowns it'll be right up your street. There's this creature who calls himself The Thought Stealer and with his three goons he's planning to steal the thoughts of everyone here until there's nothing left inside their heads."

Another clown smelt the oversized flower on his jacket. "That doesn't sound silly at all," he replied.

"It doesn't?" she gasped, surprised that someone actually believed her.

"No, of course not," he said. "Now I'm guessing you know what they look like?"

"Yes," she replied. "Three of them were dressed in dark red cloaks and the other is just a big shadow."

"So they must be in disguise," one of the clowns suggested, "otherwise you would recognise them immediately."

Annie scratched her chin. "Well I guess so…"

The clown's smile widened into a massive grin. "Because if I was a monster and wanted to be in a disguise that would fit in really well at a fairground, what do you think I'd dress up as?"

Suddenly a cold chill washed over her. Her instinct was to run, but she couldn't. All she could do was answer the question asked. "If I wanted to wear a disguise that would fit in at a fairground and wouldn't cause any suspicion, then I suppose I'd dress up as a clown," she whispered.

"Exactly," the clown rasped, removing his face that turned out to be an astonishingly realistic mask.

Annie suddenly found herself looking at a shadowy face.

Chapter thirty-one

Annie didn't have a chance to run away, or grasp her nose, as the three other clowns instantly grabbed her.

"You're hurting me," she protested; their fingers digging into her arms, pinching her skin.

"I'll do more than that," The Thought Stealer rasped. "Annabelle, you're becoming more than a mere nuisance. I should have killed you when I first had the chance, instead of ending up trying to consume that boy's thoughts."

"What?" Annie gasped.

The dark monster began to laugh. "Didn't you know? This morning I was after you. Lucky for you I grew weak waiting for you and ended up having to try and feed on that boy's thoughts instead."

Annie was stunned. "Why… why were you after me?" she stammered.

The Thought Stealer's smile took over his whole face. "Don't you know, little girl? The reason I was after you was simple. You were the only one who stood any chance of working out what would stop me."

"I was?" she whispered. "What have I got that no one else has got?"

"What have you got!" the mass of dark matter dressed as a clown bellowed. "It's what you haven't got that would have stopped me! That was why I tried to kill you in Eira's house instead of feeding on your thoughts. You're too much of a threat to me."

Annie was puzzled. "If that's so, then why did you first go after Fred inside Eira's house?"

"The boy was an easier target," The Thought Stealer explained. "He was going to be a nice little appetiser before I fed on your thoughts."

There was a brief moment of silence as what the horrible beast had said sank in. It wasn't a coincidence that she had been dragged into this adventure; she had something to do with it. But what exactly remained a mystery.

Finally Annie returned to the present. "So you're going to zombify all of the people here? Does that not bother you?"

The Thought Stealer's sharp teeth appeared behind his grin. "Why should I care? I'm made up of nothing but horrible, evil, wicked thoughts. There isn't a single thing inside me that would make me feel remorse," he growled. "And when the fireworks begin as planned, the light they give off will provide the light the Thinking Crystal needs to snatch the thoughts from every single person here."

"You're horrible," she spat.

He laughed. "I'm horrible? Oh, no, you and all of the people on this planet are horrible."

"That's not true," Annie argued.

"Of course it is," he explained. "Because if it wasn't for the horrible thoughts that every person on this planet thinks from time to time, then I would never have existed. I am merely a by-product of human nature. Even you have helped create me."

"You're lying!" she insisted.

The Thought Stealer laughed. "Oh no? So you have never had horrible, envious thoughts about other children in your school?"

"No!" she said in defiance.

"Yes you do!" The Thought Stealer laughed. "You hate it when they talk about when their parents take them to a theme park or even the zoo. Hearing them chat about it makes your toes curl with envy, because that's what you want more than anything in the world – to have your mother and father spend time with you. But you can never have that because they're dead!"

The Thought Stealer continued. "I am made up of the horrible feelings that consume you every time your aunt is late picking you up from school."

"That's not true!" Annie argued again.

"Yes it is," he hissed. "You hate yourself for it, the thoughts that go around inside your head when you wait outside school for your aunt and have to watch all of the other children being picked up by their mums and dads. Envy and jealousy well up inside, thinking how unfair it is that you're the only person who isn't picked up by her parents.

"You hate it that every child gets to go home with their mums and dads whereas all you can do is dream about your parents," The Thought Stealer taunted. "Only in your dreams do you see your mother, who'll sit on the end of your bed and read to you or stroke your hair, and only in your thoughts do you see your father."

"You're lying!" Annie shouted again.

"No, Annabelle, I'm not," the brute sneered. "You also hate it when children argue with their parents. Inside you resent those children because they don't know how lucky they are. They take their parents for granted, whereas you'd give up the world for just one minute with your mother and father."

The Thought Stealer walked around the young girl. "But those aren't the worst thoughts that bounce around inside your head. The worst thing that I've fed on is your ability to lie so easily."

Annie struggled. "You're wrong!" she snarled with a defiant smile. "I never lie!"

"No?" The Thought Stealer laughed, breathing in and seemingly feeding on the rage coming from the ten-year-old girl. "You lie every time you tell someone that you don't believe in ghosts."

"I don't believe in them – they're ridiculous!" she argued. "I believe in science!"

The Thought Stealer smiled. "That's not true… is it? It's not that you don't believe in ghosts, it's that your heart won't allow it. Because to believe in ghosts you would have to come to terms with one fact," he laughed. "If ghosts exist then you would have to come to terms with the truth that maybe your parents don't love you. Because why else would their ghosts not come and visit you?"

Annie struggled; The Thought Stealer had dragged up the one thing she hated about herself. Although she loved her aunt so much, she couldn't help but miss her mother and father like crazy. It was as though a big mum and dad shaped piece was missing from her heart and because of this she felt envious of anyone who got to spend time with their parents. She would never argue with them. She would just cuddle them.

And The Thought Stealer was right; she would give up the world for just one minute to live that for real. That would be all that she needed, just to know how it felt to be held in her parents' arms.

"How do you know that?" Annie finally demanded.

"Because those thoughts are a part of me, since I was created by the horrible side of human nature," The Thought Stealer explained.

Suddenly Annie stopped fighting. She hadn't believed it when Eira had told her earlier that day, but The Thought Stealer actually was the embodiment of everything that was bad about her and everyone else who lives on the planet.

Thoughts of wanting to steal sweets from a candy shop, thoughts of wanting to kick someone in the shins, thoughts of pretending to be ill to stay off work, thoughts of not wanting to eat greens, thoughts of wanting to rob a bank and not clean your teeth before bed. These were some of the thoughts that people had from time to time and she was looking at what they'd created.

At that moment Annie knew what The Thought Stealer was. He was a part of everyone on the planet – including herself. He was the horrible side of human nature and as long as that existed, a being like The Thought Stealer would exist.

The Thought Stealer pulled away the cylinder containing the helium gas and exposed the large Thinking Crystal in a hole dug underneath. He then turned to the clowns. "Take her away. Drain her mind dry as a reward for your loyalty," he said. "And this time don't let her escape."

"Very good, master," one of the clowns grovelled, before leading Annie through the crowded fairground.

As Annie was being pushed the mysterious voice returned. *Annabelle,* it whispered, *you're the only one who can stop this and you don't have much time.*

Annie's heart sank. She didn't believe the voice. *Help me!* her mind cried. *How can I stop him?*

Search inside yourself, the voice said. *To any other child it would be impossible to work it out, but to you it's simple.*

Annie began to cry inside. *What's the answer?* her mind yelled, her eyes searching the immediate area. She needed her *Eureka!* moment.

There were people everywhere. Some were on the rides; others were standing chatting and playing about. But what her eyes were drawn to were the two children standing next to a small ride, arguing over a toffee apple.

It was a girl and a boy, possibly brother and sister, no older than eight or nine. The girl had the toffee apple and the boy was trying to yank it out of her hands.

"It's mine!" the girl shrieked.

"I don't care!" the boy fired back. "What are you going to do, go crying to Mum like the last time?"

"No," the girl argued, right before she kicked her elder brother in the shins. He yelped and let go of the treat.

The girl used this to her advantage though, as she whacked the boy over the top of the head with the toffee apple, causing him to drop to his knees in pain.

"Maybe you should complain to Mum about me," the girl said, grinning. She then took a big bite out of her prize, the toffee apple.

Seeing this, Annie's heart missed a beat. She couldn't believe it. *She'd just witnessed the simplest thing that she believed in.*

But before she could think any more about the revelation, she was prodded in the back by one of the clowns. "I'm going to enjoy eating your thoughts," the clown teased, licking his lips with his dark shadow of a tongue. He then prodded her in the back, making her walk towards the dark grass behind the rides, where she would be hidden from view in the shadows.

"The moment the fireworks start, the Thinking Crystal will suck everyone's minds dry. Our master will then enjoy feeding on the horrible thoughts that have been stolen," the clown said. "And there'll be nothing that you can do about it."

Annie didn't reply, because she knew how to stop the horrid dark beast and his vile goons. The apple had reminded her of Sir Isaac Newton.

How could I have been so stupid? It's so simple! she thought, stumbling through the fairground. *The answer's been staring me in the face all day. The only way to stop The Thought Stealer is science. Every action has an equal and opposite reaction to be exact!*

In that moment she understood why The Thought Stealer thought she was the only one who could stop him. Unlike other children, her mind wasn't clouded by a belief in ghosts and magic. She thought about science and nothing else.

Chapter thirty-two

As Annie was being pushed past the dodgems she looked at the small cars whizzing around, bumping into each other to the sound of music and the occasional loud siren.

The flashing lights and activity got her thinking. She turned to the clowns. "Hey, catch me if you can!" she baited, tugging herself free from the clowns' grip.

Annie swiftly dashed away and, more stupid than a child running out into the road without looking, raced into the middle of the dodgems ride, causing the small cars to career out of the way to avoid knocking her over. They crashed into one another as the girl slipped over on the shiny metal surface whilst trying to hurry across to the other side.

On all fours, she looked round and saw that the three clowns had followed her onto the ride. But wearing over sized silly red boots, they weren't as agile as the small girl in the shorts and sweater. Annie was able to jump out of the way of the oncoming vehicles, whilst the clowns were knocked over.

To an onlooker it was like watching a circus act.

Annie didn't stop to watch and laugh though, as she continued to dance in between the dodgems that were whizzing out of the way to avoid knocking her over.

She sped across the ride and out the other side, before jumping down onto the grass and looking around. But she didn't stay there for long once one of the clowns appeared from the ride scruffy and roughed up.

"I'm going to tear you to pieces!" he growled.

"These guys don't give up," she muttered, dashing off through the crowds in a bid to lose them.

She ran as hard as she could for the ride that was closest. But when she looked up and saw that she'd arrived at the ghost house, she muttered, "Great… ghosts, ghouls, vampires and mummies. Why can't I go for more than two minutes without running into a monster?"

Annie quickly looked over her shoulder and saw that the clowns were in hot pursuit. "Rats," she muttered, before charging past the ride attendant, who screamed at her for not paying.

The moment Annie was inside she let out a scream, as a plastic skeleton fell down from the dark in front of her. Her heart hammering away, she brushed it aside and continued deeper inside the ride.

Within several moments though Annie became disorientated by the green flashing lights and thick white smoke hanging in the air. "Come on," she urged, searching for a way out.

But there seemed to be no end to the horrible maze, because instead of finding the back door, around each corner she turned she was greeted by either a skeleton hanging in the air or a vampire that popped out of a coffin, its sharp teeth ready to sink deep into her neck.

Regardless of this, she pressed on and suddenly received a shock when a clown jumped out in front of her. "Come here!" he snarled, trying to grab her.

Annie was fast though, dropping to her knees and sliding through his legs. She was quickly back on her feet and dashing through the dark, barging the ghosts and spiders' webs out of the way.

She then looked round and saw the clown was after her, blocking her way back out. Thinking quickly she continued upwards to the second level, knocking a teenage couple over in the process.

"Hey!" the two people cried, falling on their backsides.

"Sorry!" Annie yelled back, continuing up the creaky stairs that would have been better placed in a haunted mansion.

She swiftly looked round again and noticed the clown was snapping at her heels. "Give me a break," she panted, fighting her way through the cobwebs and smoke before darting for a door that read *No exit.*

She kicked it open and raced out onto the roof of the ride. But as she got to the edge of the roof she groaned, "Ah no."

There was no way off.

She was about to dash for the other side to see if there was a way off when one of the clowns appeared, blocking the way.

"You're trapped, little girl," the clown snarled, its smile looking very sinister.

Annie backed up onto the edge, unsure what to do. She was two levels up and couldn't jump without risking a broken leg.

Chapter thirty-three

But then she spied a familiar face in the crowds below. It was Fred; he was looking around for her.

"Fred!" she yelled, backing away from the clown. "I'm up here!"

Fred looked up. "Annie, what are you doing up there?"

"There's no time to explain!" she replied, turning to the two other clowns who had appeared on the roof before turning back to the boy. "I need to get off here!"

Thinking fast, Fred looked around and then dashed through the crowd to where The Thought Stealer had been handing out balloons filled with helium gas. There were about thirty of them hanging in the air tied down by pieces of string, which were attached to the bottom of the cylinder.

With The Thought Stealer nowhere to be seen, Fred was able to quickly pull the cylinder over to the side of the ghost house and bind the pieces of string together.

"Annie!" Fred shouted. "Grab hold of these!"

Fred set the balloons free from the cylinder and together they rose into the air.

"I hate cutting these things fine!" she gasped, the clowns crowding round her.

The moment before they got her though, the balloons passed her and she grabbed the strings that were attached to them.

The result was absolutely incredible.

The balloons had such upward lift they pulled her high into the air, away from the three clowns.

Annie held on tight, too scared to look down – since she was petrified of heights – until she passed over the helter-skelter. Confident that she wouldn't break a leg she let go of the strings and fell onto the ride, which looked like a fifty foot high tower with a massive slide wrapped around it. The people waiting to take the spiral slide down to the bottom had shock on their faces.

"Sorry to push in," she grinned to the people, before grabbing a mat and jumping onto the slide. She whizzed down to the bottom, where she was met by Fred.

"Annie, are you okay?" he asked.

Annie just nodded as she grabbed Fred by the arm and dragged him through the masses of people.

"We need to hurry," she panted. "The moment the fireworks begin the light that they emit will cause the Thinking Crystal to start sucking people's minds dry."

"That's where the light's going to come from?" Fred asked.

"Yeah, I can't believe I didn't think of that – it's so obvious," Annie panted whilst racing across the road that divided the green where the fair was and the green where the fireworks were going to take off from.

But the pair got half way to their destination when it happened!

A small red dot shot out from the ground and into the dark sky above. It seemed to hang there for a lifetime, before there was a flash of red light which was followed by a *bang!*

It was the first firework of the display, which erupted, lighting the sky in a fountain of red.

"Oh, no," Annie muttered, watching a second firework shoot into the air and explode with a bang, spraying green particles over the dark canvas. "We're too late."

Annie stood, stunned, while the fireworks shot into the sky with a rhythm that increased as the seconds ticked by.

There were brilliant flashes of green, red, purple, orange and yellow. The fireworks exploded into different shapes. Some burst into mushroom shapes whilst others opened up into rings of light or fell like sparkling raindrops.

Annie's mind raced. She then looked over at the fairground and saw something that made her mouth drop.

The Thought Stealer was standing in the middle of the fair holding the Thinking Crystal above his head.

Seeing this, Annie knew that it had begun. The crystal was sucking the thoughts out of everyone's minds and storing them inside. Because The Thought Stealer was holding the crystal, he was able to consume the nasty ones, before discarding the rest.

She quickly pinched her nose closed whilst looking round at all of the people. Fred did the same.

The people all around were standing there completely still, just like Fred earlier that day. Their bodies were as stiff as boards, their eyes were wide open and their thoughts were being sucked out through their noses.

With the horror happening around her, Annie wanted to scream. She knew the answer, but it was too late.

Suddenly the ghostly voice returned. *Annabelle,* it said, *it's not too late to stop this. Trust your judgement.*

"How?" she yelled, looking out over the headland at the harbour way down below. The breakwater stretched out into the sea and the lighthouse twinkled at the end.

But then, spying the lighthouse, the answer fell into place!

The realisation that she had worked everything out made her heart skip a beat. She knew how to stop The Thought Stealer; the clues had been there ever since she was at the coastguard station!

She turned to Fred. "Try and find an adult who isn't a zombie to stop the fireworks. Without their

166

light the Thinking Crystal is harmless," she explained. "And don't go near the fireworks yourself – they're very dangerous!"

Fred nodded and darted off towards where the fireworks were taking off from.

"Good luck!" Annie yelled to the boy. She then raced through the crowds of zombies until she found several teenage boys standing like statues. One of them was holding his bike.

"Sorry, but I need to borrow this," she muttered, relieving the boy of his bike. She then jumped onto it, peddled out of the fairground and down the hill towards the harbour, holding one hand on the handlebar and the other over her nose.

As she did, she glanced at The Thought Stealer and realised she didn't have much time. He was growing in size as he fed on all of the bad thoughts of the people around, including his three ugly goons, consuming them whole!

Chapter thirty-four

Annie cycled so hard that sweat was trickling off her forehead and it felt like a fire was burning within her legs. But she didn't care; she knew all of the answers. They were contained in the small lighthouse at the end of the breakwater. All she was now worried about was whether she'd make it there in time.

She had made it down to the harbour as quickly as a cat and was racing along the walkway, past the canoeing building and the lifeboat station and onto the breakwater.

The breakwater was a long mass of boulders and concrete that had the harbour to its left and the open water of Torbay to its right. There was a flat walkway that led right out to the small lighthouse at the end – just under a mile away.

Annie put the bike into top gear and raced over the top of the breakwater to the end. In the dark the small flashlight on the handlebars cut a beam in front, enabling her to go as fast as her tired legs would allow.

As she cycled, she looked over and noticed the fireworks were continuing to light the sky above the headland at the opposite side of the harbour. There were flashes of red, green, yellow and purple; all were swiftly accompanied by loud *bangs!* The Thought Stealer was also there, growing into a massive black cloud. He was becoming more powerful. He was approaching critical mass!

Annie wasn't disheartened by this though and continued to peddle, before finally pulling up to the old lighthouse, which was a white metal cigar-shaped building with a circular glass window running around the top that had a rotating red light inside. Streaks of rust and seagull droppings, which covered the whole of the edifice, made it look a sorry sight.

She quickly discarded the bike, raced up to the door and with her heart throbbing and hands trembling pulled it open; the hinges creaked in protest.

But the moment she tentatively stepped inside she stopped dead in her tracks, because standing there under the dim light hanging from the ceiling, waiting for her, was a figure draped in a dark red cloak. It was standing hunched, with only a wooden cane preventing it from collapsing.

"Annabelle, you may not pass," the figure wheezed from under the hood covering its face. "My master will not allow it."

The figure then removed its hood and Annie received a massive shock, because underneath was the face of Eira Flynn.

Chapter thirty-five

Annie's shock quickly wore off and was replaced by an urge to be sick. She pinched her nose before looking at the face of the person who she thought had been turned into a zombie earlier that day. But now she knew that wasn't the case and she instantly realised why. "Vincent," she whispered.

Vincent cackled, before removing the face of Eira Flynn, which was a very convincing rubber mask. Underneath was a dark shadow.

Annie looked closely and, although he was obviously a horrible Thought Person, his appearance was much different to his brother, The Thought Stealer. His features were haggard, tired and worn. The bags under his dark eyes and wrinkled texture of his face made him look a hundred years old.

Annie didn't move. "You killed Eira Flynn, didn't you?" she whispered.

Vincent just nodded.

"She managed to stop you from completing your plan of achieving critical mass and becoming all powerful. Instead you were left weakened and that's why you're confined to a wheelchair and have to breathe through a face mask. I'm guessing that after you killed her and were left weakened, you assumed her identity for many years," she said.

"That's very good, my girl," Vincent wheezed. "If that troublesome woman hadn't have stopped me, I would have consumed enough rotten thoughts to become as powerful as a monster, but instead I was left in a frail and feeble state and confined to a wheelchair. Assuming Eira's identity was the ideal way to survive in this horrible state without arousing suspicion."

Although Annie's heart was racing, she was angry with herself that she hadn't taken notice of the clues before. The pages of the book in the library had been ripped out by Vincent and Annie guessed it was entitled, *How to Stop a Horrible Thought Person.* Vincent obviously didn't want anyone else knowing how to stop him and his brother.

Furthermore, when she saw the dark matter come out of Eira's mouth, she had presumed it was The Thought Stealer. But it wasn't, it was Vincent. The exertion of The Thought Stealer's attack on Fred and herself must have inadvertently weakened the frail horrible Thought Person and he needed to get his energy back somewhere quiet.

She then looked to Vincent. "The Thought Stealer didn't follow us to your house; he came to visit you."

Again Vincent nodded.

"And by telling us that long-winded account of what a Thought Person was and what happened in the battle between yourself and Miss Flynn – which

I now suspect is far from the truth – you kept us at the house long enough for The Thought Stealer to attack us," Annie continued, "since you were too weak to defeat us yourself."

Once more Vincent nodded. "You're very clever, my girl. It was only a shame The Thought Stealer didn't kill you this morning when you were taking an early morning stroll."

Annie looked from Vincent to the cylindrical chamber running up the centre of the lighthouse, which contained the mechanism that operated the rotating light at the top.

Vincent hobbled towards her, aided by a walking stick. "How did you work out that this place held the key to stopping The Thought Stealer?"

Annie backed off. "Simple," she replied, keeping an eye on him, making sure he wasn't going to get too close. "Science. You see, The Thought Stealer is made up of nothing but horrible thoughts. He's like the negative pole of a magnet. When I was thinking of what would destroy him, I was thinking of complicated things, when the answer was simple. Sir Isaac Newton's Third Law of Motion to be precise."

She paused for effect for several moments before continuing, "*Every action has an equal and opposite reaction.* Up and down. Black and white. Positive and negative and so on," the girl explained. "With this in mind, if a being was created out of bad thoughts, then Newton's Third Law states that its opposite must also be created. For there to be a being made of nothing but evil, science tells us that there must be a being made up of nothing but good."

Annie explained: "Hope, friendship, kindness, happiness, the thought of helping someone or telling someone that you're sorry. There's a being that's made of all of these thoughts."

Before Vincent could speak, Annie continued. "But you already know that!" she declared. "Because you managed to find a way to trap all of the discarded good thoughts inside this lighthouse, keeping them out of your way."

The feeble villain nodded as he tried to advance on the young girl. But she was quicker, moving out of the way and keeping her distance, safe in the knowledge that in a circular room she could never be backed into a corner.

Annie then spoke. "So how did you trap all of the good thoughts?"

Vincent grinned. "Oh it was very simple in the end," he rasped. "Many years ago my brother and I found a very special crystal."

"A black coloured Thinking Crystal?" Annie whispered, realising that The Thought Stealer had lied earlier about only finding yellow coloured crystals.

Vincent nodded. "Exactly. It was only small, so it didn't suck good thoughts out of people's heads. But that didn't matter, since the light of the lighthouse allowed it to attract good thoughts that had escaped from people's heads and trapped them inside. It stopped a good Thought Person from roaming free. The Good Thought Person was effectively imprisoned inside the crystal, unable to stop us."

Annie was sickened. Vincent and The Thought Stealer had a way of capturing and imprisoning every single discarded good thought. She decided that to free all of the good thoughts, she would have to destroy the black crystal.

Annie was about to ask more about the stone, when Vincent changed the subject. "So how did you find this place?" he asked.

Annie rubbed her chin, trying to look all knowledgeable. "When I realised that The Thought Stealer had an opposite, the pieces started to fall into place. If The Thought Stealer's made up of dark matter, his opposite must be made up of light matter, and if The Thought Stealer's cold, his opposite must be hot," she explained.

"But that doesn't explain why you came here," Vincent wheezed, becoming weaker with every breath he took.

"Oh, it does!" Annie fired back. "When I was at the coastguard station, the watch officer said the lighthouse was the hottest place in the whole of Brixham."

Annie looked over at the metal cylindrical shaft running up the centre of the lighthouse, before feeling the warmth coming from within it. Trapped inside was a Thought Person that was made up of nothing but good thoughts. If she could free it, then it would be able to stop The Thought Stealer; that she was sure. The good side of human nature was so much stronger than the bad side.

She looked to Vincent's feeble form. "You're weak and you won't be able to stop me from freeing the light that's trapped inside."

"You're right, my battle with Eira Flynn left me weak and feeble," Vincent said, breathing with difficulty. "But my intention wasn't to stop you... It was to distract you."

Suddenly Annie froze. The time she'd spent talking to Vincent had been time that The Thought Stealer had spent growing stronger. She should have freed the good Thought Person from within the lighthouse earlier.

Realising her mistake, she barged past Vincent, knocking him over, and darted over to the hatch that allowed access to inside the centre of the lighthouse.

But as she was about to pull the handle and open the hatch, she became aware of something!

The air inside the small structure had turned very cold indeed.

Chapter thirty-six

Goosebumps appeared on her arms like a thousand tiny mountains and the hairs on the back of her neck suddenly stood to attention. She looked at her breath: the grey vapour hung in the air, before disappearing.

Slowly, she looked round and, to her horror, standing in the doorway was The Thought Stealer.

Looking at The Thought Stealer's new appearance robbed Annie of her breath. He was stronger and more menacing. Instead of appearing as a shadow, he was now completely real.

The ghastly thoughts of the hundreds of people he had just fed on had made him so strong. His body was now like a human shaped mass of crude oil, thick and viscous.

The Thought Stealer tilted his head back and drew a deep breath. "Ahh," he snarled, the rawness still in his voice, "so strong."

Annie stepped back, not taking her eyes off The Thought Stealer as he moved inside the lighthouse, his feet making the ground tremble with every step. He then looked to Vincent, who was now on his knees. "Brother," Vincent wheezed, "she overpowered me."

"You are weak and you've outlived your usefulness!" The Thought Stealer growled, before drawing in a deep breath.

In an instant, Vincent's dark form was sucked through the air and into The Thought Stealer's mouth, until all that was left of the feeble creature was his red cloak and walking stick lying on the floor in a pile. One moment he was there, the next he was gone. Vincent simply added to The Thought Stealer's power.

Annie backed off again.

The Thought Stealer laughed. "Annabelle, you are next and don't think that your best friend, Fred, will come and rescue you. I have already stolen all of his thoughts," he growled. "He came so close to getting the organisers to stop the fireworks."

Annie's heart sank. *Not Fred,* she thought.

The monster continued to laugh. "I also fed on the thoughts of your aunt."

Hearing this Annie almost cried. "You wicked creature!" she hissed. "They did nothing wrong."

"Don't concern yourself with their minds being sucked dry!" he exclaimed. "The end for you is very close now."

Annie backed onto the hatch and grabbed hold of the handle. "So what do you plan to do next?" she demanded, trying to pull the handle down. But it was rusted tight.

"I will enslave everyone in this world. If anybody wishes to stand in my way, they'll die or suffer the same fate as all of the other Thought People, trapped in eternal torture and agony," he explained, raising his arm and pointed his horrible bony finger at her.

Annie continued to wrestle with the handle, but it wouldn't budge.

"You're so predictable," The Thought Stealer tormented, his fingers extending like spaghetti and wrapping around her legs.

Annie instantly let go of the handle and tried to break free from his grip. But it was no good and she was suddenly turned upside down and pulled up so that she was hanging in the air.

"I'm not going to steal your thoughts," he hissed. "For all of the trouble you caused me I'm going to take pleasure in killing you."

He then carried Annie outside and dangled her over the side of the breakwater.

"This isn't good," she muttered to herself, looking down and noticing that it was a long drop to the surface of the water, since the breakwater was made up of piles and piles of massive boulders.

He then dropped her and her stomach did a somersault as she fell through the air before hitting the water with a splash.

Again the cold liquid took her breath away and stabbed at her body like a thousand needles.

Her head broke the surface and she quickly looked up. The Thought Stealer suddenly transformed from his human shape and into a cloud of dark matter. But this time he was different. The cloud was darker, larger and colder. Bolts of lightening flashed from inside, which were swiftly followed by the crackle of thunder.

He swept down, picked Annie out of the water and flung her into the air.

"Ah!" she screamed, feeling as though her stomach was about to go through her feet.

The sensation lasted for several moments until she finally fell back into the water with a massive splash and once again the cold water enveloped her.

The moment her head broke the surface she watched The Thought Stealer dive straight into the water in the middle of the harbour and disappear under the surface.

Annie had a bad feeling about what was about to happen next, so she frantically swam towards the base of the breakwater.

And she almost made it when the most horrid thing happened. The water around her began to tug at her tired and worn body.

A lot like what had happened earlier that day in the caves, it felt like massive tentacles had wrapped themselves around her legs and arms.

With the water tugging at her body, she looked round. But the moment she did, she wished she'd kept looking forward, because an enormous whirlpool had formed in the middle of the harbour. The Thought Stealer was spinning round very fast at the bed of the harbour, creating the same motion as water disappearing down the plug hole in a bathtub.

The water circled rapidly, pulling everything towards it. Boats were suddenly tugging against their moorings and seagulls floating on the surface took to the sky.

Fearing she would be dragged to her death, she swam through the water, which was pulling her exhausted body towards the whirlpool. But in no time her arms started to ache and the current began to drag her away from the breakwater, which loomed over her like a massive dark wall.

It was so close, but she couldn't reach it!

The whirlpool in the middle of the harbour grew larger and stronger. Suddenly boats were ripped from their moorings and pulled into the massive whirlpool. There was a crunch of tortured wood as the vessels – including the sunken tall ship – were smashed to pieces at the bottom.

The current around Annie became stronger and stronger. It had been a long and tiring day and now she no longer had the energy to fight against the swell. Her arms burned, her body was exhausted and she was completely drained. Water shot up her nose causing her to cough and splutter.

Come on, you can do it! her mind shrieked. But it was too much; she couldn't fight it any more!

Although the rocks at the bottom of the breakwater were just out of arm's reach, she knew she would never grasp them. She gave in and allowed the swell to wrap itself around her body and drag her towards the deadly whirlpool in the middle.

Chapter thirty-seven

Suddenly, out of nowhere, a hand wrapped itself around Annie's wrist and held her against the pull of the water, stopping her from being dragged to her death.

So fatigued, she could barely manage to look up. But when she did, what she saw came as a complete surprise. Standing on the rocks, where the breakwater met the surface, was Fred.

He grinned. "You pick the strangest times to go for a swim!"

Annie was too tired to reply and just allowed Fred to drag her out of the water to safety. The moment she was out of the water, tiredness hit – her body feeling like a sack of potatoes – and she collapsed into his arms.

"I thought The Thought Stealer had stolen all of your thoughts," Annie managed to whisper.

"He thought he had," Fred joked, suddenly standing perfectly still and opening his eyes as wide as golf balls. "Quite convincing, don't you think?"

Annie managed a weak smile, before allowing herself to melt into his arms. She had never been happier to see another soul in her entire life. "How did you find me?" she asked.

"The Thought Stealer was pretty difficult to miss," he explained. "It's not everyday you have one of the worse looking stormy clouds known to man hovering over the end of Brixham breakwater."

"Good point," Annie replied.

Fred then looked over at the harbour. "What's going on?"

"It's The Thought Stealer," Annie muttered. "He's out of control. We need to get to the lighthouse as quickly as we can."

Annie then looked up, but from where they were on the rocks, which sloped up to the top of the breakwater to where the lighthouse was standing, it seemed like a mountain.

Even though it seemed an impossible climb, with tiredness gripping every muscle and bone in her body, there was a tiny voice in the back of her mind stopping her from curling up into a ball and falling asleep. Instead, it was demanding that she kept going.

As Annie listened to the voice, she realised it wasn't the ghostly voice she'd heard throughout the day – it was different. It sounded like her mother's voice sounded in her dreams. *Don't give up,* it whispered. *Darling Annabelle, don't ever give up.*

Not only was this voice telling her not to give up, but she seemed to muster a small amount of strength that she didn't have a few moments earlier. Her arms and legs stopped aching and a surge of energy came from nowhere. She looked up at the lighthouse and it now didn't seem so far away.

She pulled herself to her feet and stared out over the harbour. It was a scene of devastation. Boats were still being pulled relentlessly into the whirlpool, before being smashed to pieces.

She turned to Fred. "We need to get to the lighthouse."

The young boy nodded and the pair clambered up the stones towards the lighthouse as fast as their feet would allow.

Several moments later and Fred stopped, before looking round. "Annie!" he yelled, "I think we have a problem!"

Annie was relentlessly stumbling over the coarse stones near the top, her energy seemingly coming from nowhere, when she looked round. But what she saw made her mouth drop.

The monster had emerged from beneath the water and was now hovering in a cloud above the destruction he'd caused. Although the whirlpool had stopped, there wasn't a single boat left afloat. The harbour had been stripped bare.

The Thought Stealer suddenly turned to the two children and flew straight for them.

"We need to hurry!" she yelled to Fred, grabbing him by the arm and dragging him over the final boulders so that they were again standing in front of the lighthouse.

But no sooner was Fred standing there than The Thought Stealer swept down and lifted him into the air.

"No!" Annie screamed, trying to grab the boy's leg. But he was pulled out of arm's reach too quickly.

The dark beast swung Fred around like a shot put and slung him into the air. The boy let out a horrible shriek as he was propelled through the night time sky, before hitting the water with a giant splash.

Annie looked up to The Thought Stealer, who was hovering in front of her. "I'm so strong," he hissed. "Nothing can stop me."

Annie didn't say anything and instead turned and ran for the lighthouse that was merely feet away. She was fast and the moment before the shadowy monster flew for her she dived through the doorway, slammed the door shut and quickly locked it.

But with no time to catch her breath, she suddenly felt The Thought Stealer pull at the handle.

"He'll have the door off its hinges in no time," she muttered, running to the cylindrical structure in the middle of the lighthouse and grabbing the handle of the small hatch that gave access to the hollow space inside.

It took no time at all for The Thought Stealer to pull the door off its hinges. "Do you think that could stop me?" he growled, easily discarding the door before marching inside.

"This time, Annabelle," he continued, "there's no escape for you."

But at the same time The Thought Stealer flew straight for her, Annie pulled down on the handle, opened the hatch and dived into the small confined space.

Annie didn't take long to see the small black crystal resting on the floor. With her heart racing and hands trembling, she quickly grabbed it before throwing it on the floor as hard as she could.

Chapter thirty-eight

What happened next was utterly mind-blowing. As soon as the crystal shattered, a brilliant white light erupted from within the broken pieces. The force of the light escaping from its prison knocked Annie off her feet before it shot out through the hatch and smashed into The Thought Stealer's form. It propelled the horrible beast into the opposite wall with a *thud!*

Annie watched in stunned silence as the beam of light wrapped itself around The Thought Stealer's body like a snake strangling its prey.

The Thought Stealer fought back with such power and strength. He wrestled with the light, crashing into the walls and rolling on the floor. It was turning into a monstrous battle.

"You'll never stop me!" The Thought Stealer yelled whilst fighting with the light that circled him tighter and tighter.

"I'm the most powerful thing on this planet!" he yelled, his arms flapping and thrashing wildly – trying to break free.

He roared and cried, continuing to crash into the walls, before rolling on the ground.

But the beam of light was like a coil of rope, tightening its grip on the mass of dark matter.

Moments from death, The Thought Stealer let out a shriek right before there was a flash of intense light.

Although Annie put her hand over her eyes, the light still filtered through. It was so bright!

Suddenly there was a roar like thunder, which shook the lighthouse, causing the glass at the top to shatter and rain down on top of her. She put her arms over her head as a shield.

"Ahhh!" Annie shrieked, fearing this was the end as large cracks then appeared in the stone floor.

The rumbling, shaking and rattling, which made it seem like the worst ever earthquake was occurring inside the lighthouse, continued for several more moments before they suddenly stopped, leaving only silence to fill the air.

Too scared to even breathe, Annie finally pulled her hand away from her eyes and looked at what was in front of her.

Standing there was a human shaped mass of light. It was beautiful, just like an angel.

The mass of light changed into a bright cloud and floated into the air before saying in the ghostly voice she'd heard so many times that day, "Thank you."

Annie was stunned. "It was you who was speaking to me all day?" she asked, whilst emerging through the hatchway.

"Yes," it replied.

"Then why didn't you just lead me straight here, instead of giving me clues that took me on a wild goose chase?" Annie asked, getting straight to the point.

188

The light circled the inside of the small lighthouse. "If I told you everything this morning, because you didn't believe in ghosts and monsters you wouldn't have believed me. You simply would have dismissed all of this as nonsense and got on with your day, leaving The Thought Stealer to carry out his horrible plan unopposed. The only way that you would have believed in Thought People to the point that you were in a position to stop The Thought Stealer was to discover the truth for yourself. That's why I only led you in the right direction and didn't tell you everything."

"But how did you know to contact me?" Annie asked, so many questions swimming around in her mind.

"Because I am made up of discarded and forgotten good thoughts, including yours – you have so many," the light explained. "And because of that I knew you could help me stop The Thought Stealer."

Annie smiled.

A smile formed in the middle of the mass of light, right before it disappeared out of the doorway and fished Fred out of the water. It placed him down next to her before shooting into the air and illuminating the sky over the fairground.

"You look wet through," Annie commented, noticing that Fred's clothes were drenched and his brown hair was matted to his head.

Fred looked over at the headland across the harbour. "Who was that?"

"That's the embodiment of everything that's good about human nature," Annie explained. "It's the exact opposite of The Thought Stealer and Vincent."

"And what's it doing?" he asked.

"I think it's returning the thoughts that The Thought Stealer stole," she replied.

"And where's that horrible Thought Person now?" he asked.

"Gone," she explained.

Chapter thirty-nine

Three hours had passed before Annie, Fred and her aunt had made it back to the campsite.

Aunt Grace had no recollection of the events that saw all of her thoughts being stolen by The Thought Stealer, before the mysterious mass of bright light returned them along with the thoughts of everyone else. All she felt was as though she'd lost half an hour of her memory.

Annie and Fred, however, were exhausted. It had been a very long and eventful day, and before Fred wandered off to bed he swiftly told Annie that he would call for her early in the morning so that they could spend the day doing nothing but relaxing at the beach, eating ice cream and swimming in the sea.

Although Annie felt extremely happy that she'd found someone she could call a friend, what The Thought Stealer had told her left her feeling unsettled. Had he been right? Was the reason she didn't believe in ghosts because she was frightened that if she did believe in ghosts, she'd have to ask whether her parents loved her? She felt stupid for thinking this... she was a ten-year-old girl and she was questioning why the ghosts of her parents hadn't visited. But the more she tried to say that she was too old to ask this question, the more the thought ate away at her.

As she sat down on a comfortable chair outside her caravan and her aunt disappeared inside to prepare two glasses of lemonade, Annie's mind started to race. What she'd witnessed that day got her wondering. If a creature like The Thought Stealer could exist, then there was a good chance that things such as ghost could also exist.

If this is true, she wondered, *then why haven't Mum and Dad come to visit me... surely if they loved me they would have tried everything they could to come and see me, or sent some sort of sign at least.*

The more she thought about this, the more downtrodden she felt. "What's wrong with me?" she whispered. "Why wouldn't Mum and Dad want to come and see me?"

"What's that?" Aunt Grace asked, appearing at the door, not fully hearing what Annie had said.

"Nothing," Annie replied, rubbing a tear from her eye.

Aunt Grace saw this. "Hey, what's wrong?" she asked in the comforting tone that made Annie love her so much.

The young girl smiled with embarrassment, whilst taking a glass of lemonade from her aunt. "It's nothing."

Aunt Grace sat down in the chair next to her niece before putting her arm round her and drawing her in for a hug, which instantly made Annie feel good. "Annie, I know you well enough to know when something's up," Aunt Grace said. "So what's bothering you?"

Annie took a sip of her drink, which felt cold against the warm night air, as something inside her urged her to tell her aunt what was on her mind. She put it down to the fact that she knew whatever she told her aunt, she'd understand.

"Aunt, do you think if Mum and Dad met me today they'd like me?" the young girl blurted out.

Aunt Grace was taken aback. "Annie," she spoke softly, "whatever makes you ask that?"

She didn't want to tell her aunt the reasons why she questioned whether her parents would like her or not, so she said, "I'm just not sure they'd like me."

"Annie, although I never really knew your dad – since your parents hadn't been married too long before they died – but I know for certain that your mum loved you more than life itself."

"But how do you know that?" Annie asked, thinking that her aunt was just trying to make her feel better.

Aunt Grace smiled. "For one, she was my younger sister and I knew her like the back of my hand, and when she first held you in her arms the look in her eyes said that she loved you," the lady explained. "It's as simple as that."

For some reason this made Annie feel slightly better.

"Furthermore," Annie's aunt continued. "When you were born, your mother said to me that she was going to be everything to you. She said that she was going to be there for you when you needed her the most. And I know it's a bit of a cliché, but she also said that she was going to be your strength when you were weak, pick you up when you were down and teach you to be a good person."

"Really, then why have I never seen –" Annie suddenly stopped herself mid-sentence.

There was a brief pause. "What do you mean by that?" Aunt Grace asked.

Annie took several moments to answer. "I found out today why I don't believe in ghosts and only believe in science. It's because to believe in ghosts would be to ask myself why Mum and Dad have never come to visit. I'm beginning to believe that maybe it's because they don't love me."

Aunt Grace smiled broadly. "Annie," she said, "not seeing the ghosts of your mum and dad doesn't mean that they don't love you. Very rarely do people see ghosts."

"Besides," Annie's aunt added, "if your mother could come and visit you from the afterlife… whichever way she could achieve it, she would do it, I assure you of that."

For some reason Annie believed her aunt and because of that, her body suddenly relaxed and felt tired… throughout the day she'd had to battle monsters, save everyone from having their thoughts stolen and contend with the question of whether her parents loved her. But all of these things had been solved and because of this, her body and mind decided it was time to rest, so she then allowed herself to fall asleep in her aunt's arms.

But as she slept, for the first time in a long time her mother wasn't the only person she dreamt about – she also dreamt about her new friend Fred. And she couldn't wait to see where their friendship would go next.

The end

ABOUT THE AUTHOR

Guy Wilson was born in Southport, grew up in Devon and now lives in Leicestershire. The Thought Stealers is his first novel; a self published piece of work.

To find out more about the author, to leave a comment about the book or to get a sneak preview of the next Annie Short adventure, entitled *Dreams and Nightmares*, you can visit his website;

www.guywilson.co.uk.